IRONY
OF
GOD

by
Ronald A. Arjune

For Alien Life here and beyond

Foreword

I would like to note that according to my schizophrenia, thoughts are changing reality in real time that you do not notice because time is not discriminating between us. Physical and mental conditions of your environment may change beyond your will because body language due to movement is being used by intelligence to control encounters with each other with time as you read or behave with differences.

Table of Contents

Chapter 1

I waited for the Coach bus in front of Green Hills for about 15 minutes then it arrived. I paid $6.10 and the last stop is at the Port Authority Bus Terminal near Times Square-41st & 8th Avenue to be exact. There were about 10 people on the bus then it dropped to 5 then rose again to about 25 to 30 as it neared Manhattan. The temperature was around 45 degrees Fahrenheit and there was a fear of paranoia of rain happening. After about 90 minutes I reached my destination. At the terminal I said hello to a homeless man and he asked me to buy him a cup of coffee with 4 sugars and a little milk and so I did, along with one for myself, the same way.

"Have a happy New Year sir," I said.

"May the Lord bless you," he said, and I headed for the number 2 train to go to my parents home in the Bronx. Outside I took a video of activity on the streets and uploaded it to Facebook. I noticed that the streets were very busy with people as I walked to 7th Avenue. I went underground to the train platform and people seemed oblivious to me. I think like they're acting like they don't know the U so they don't have to know me and tell me what they know. I suspect this is to keep God's love a secret and the fact that they use my conscience to use force.

"What's that box on your waist?" A police officer said on the street above before here.

"I'm a schizophrenic and I use it as a listening device. I built it myself and I assure you it's not a bomb."

"Someone called us that's why I'm asking you." The police officer said. "Go on your way now and don't stand there."

I was standing on the sidewalk where the train entrance was to go downstairs. Earlier I remember that someone told me that the box would be a problem and this memory is in the train but I came with the bus so how could that be true? Maybe my future and my past switched and I had some kind of an hallucinating experience.

Recently there was a truck that ran over some people in Berlin so they are on high alert. I walked underground to get the number 2 train after the incident with the officer.

The PA announced that there was a number 2 train approaching the platform and rumbled to a stop and when it arrived I boarded it.

A Chinese woman was selling DVDs and showed people what she had and when she came to me I told her I was not interested. I think the Chinese have a secret admiration for me.

"Do you have the new Star Wars movie?" Someone asked. The lady showed her that she did and she bought it for $5. Obviously it was bootleg movies because it wouldn't be out this fast on DVD. You sort of get a hint that the quality of the video would not be good although the packaging looks good. I think this is due to me selling a motor to someone my age when I was younger for $10. I took the motor from an abandoned car near where I was living and that motor was for a fan that required a lot of current from a battery which I knew the person that I sold it to would not have available to make it turn. It was a sinister thing to do but I think I was possessed and under control to do that. I found that I was always in need of money and one time my father asked me if I stole money from the room he slept in. I think I did steal his money by sleepwalking.

The train was always slow as if they never had permission from the man to repair the tracks. They're always doing track repair maybe because they cannot transform the physical by going back in time with memory. It could be a dangerous thing to go back in time to repair the tracks, who knows what could happen. You could get lost in time-space or you could injure your body by the physical that does not correspond with time-space.

As the train was arriving to 238th Street I got up from my seat and looked around as if I wondered what is this all about and what am I doing here. When the train arrived at 238th Street I went to Wakefield Paint to make some keys for a lock that I previously installed at my parents home. It's $2 or less for a key, I'm not sure. After that, I took the 16 bus and arrived at my parents home in 5 minutes and my parents greeted me when I opened the door with the keys I normally carry when I visit them. My dad was responsible with our security and he was reliable on putting good locks on the doors. For some reason he knew danger more than me-not that anybody is going to get us. He could have lived a secret life that he never told us about since my mom was always worried that he was seeing other women. Being a Postal Worker must have put him among a lot of women.

"How are you son?" My mother said. "How was your trip?"

"It was good mom, there was no traffic problem," I said. "How were you and Dad?"

"Glad to see you son." Said dad and he hugged me saying, "I love you." He sounded like he really tried to help me in life but he couldn't because of unknown conditions he couldn't say-maybe that secret life, if so.

That same night I cleared the sewer which is easily blocked. You have to push in the snake just at the opening, which is in the basement. That is where it usually gets blocked. Also, I fixed Windows update by putting a question on Microsoft community about my father's computer. Windows was unable to do updates. After two manual files were installed by me, the computer began to notify me of updates automatically again. I installed the current updates. After that I didn't feel handicapped. I went upstairs.

My mother told me she wanted to put up the valance for the drapes so I had to buy a curtain rod. I took the BX 16 bus to the hardware store which is rather scary because the blacks are watching to see how you look at them-if you have hate. They don't want to look at me in the eye because they don't want to perform a test on me. Anyway I reached the hardware store at White Plains Road and bought it and came back with the bus going the opposite direction. I also bought chandelier bulbs for the chandelier in the dining room and replaced two of them that were out. In the house, I used the ladder to climb up to the top and installed the rod for the valance and it was fixed after some calculated effort. The original mounting hardware were removed because my mother insisted on using her own blinds and this complicated things a lot. I think this attitude of having her own way was due to her college education, like it removed some of her sensitivity.

"Let me climb up and adjust it so it looks good Anthony." My mother said. She climbed up the ladder and I was concerned of her falling since normally most people would be. She adjusted the valence according to her taste and showed satisfaction with her effort. My mother gives me simple work, or should I say what looks simple, but it's always a challenge mentally not knowing how she likes things done and what she doesn't. It's as if she does not give me a chance to use my own intelligence.

"An anomaly must have changed the physical condition," I told her. After that the valance seemingly adjusted itself to look good. She laughed not knowing that I was serious with my paranoia. I was sick for many years and my mother and father were patient with my bad behavior. Now I am reasonable trying to understand the unknown with my paranoia. I reasoned that they, those who have sold their souls, love each other physically with the resonance of God and the Devil for pleasure. To do this you have to sell your soul to the devil. The love removes our nerves with our relationship and that is a test due to mental & physical contact occurring as sin. Sin is something necessary for life. The rain is a sin on an enormous scale.

I accompanied my father for dialysis on Thursday and Saturday. I would buy him a coffee just before he's done at Dunkin' Donuts so it will be warm. Transportation would call on his cell phone with the vehicle number and time of pickup just after he's done with dialysis. Dad told me it was difficult for me to accompany him but I told him it was no problem and that was because I cared and that is why it was no problem.

We watched the ball drop at Times Square on New Year's Eve on television. Just before that I took some pictures of us and posted it on Facebook. My cousins on my mother's side appreciate the post on Facebook-they like to see Mom and Dad. Most of my father's family stayed in Guyana and didn't come to America but they never gave me a reason why. When 2017 reached we had some champagne and went to bed.

When I woke up that Sunday morning my mother made breakfast because I was going back to Rockland where I lived. I took my mental health medications and prepared my bags to go back on the bus and train. I packed some black cake for Patricia who lived where I live. When it was time to go I kissed my mother goodbye and shook my father's hand and wished them well. I felt sad leaving my father who has diabetes and vision problems. With my schizophrenia I could not live home with them because I would decompensate. I might suspect them of evil and want to harm them.

"Have a safe trip home," My mother said at the front door. "I'm going to look out the window till I see the bus."

I must figure out what to instruct the computer or system to restore my father and make him recover physically. There is a small Qbasic computer program on his IBM ps1 I made using the random number statement that looped with GOTO to repeat. It is my hope that the output numbers would cause his recovery by using the system as it printed on the Tandy DMP250 printer.

The Bx16 bus took a short time to arrive and I boarded it and headed for 238th Street and White Plains Road. After going up the stairs I entered the number 2 train which took a long time to get to Times Square. There was a deaf woman begging for money on the train and I gave her $2. A man was giving out sandwiches on the train and requested a small donation. At 42nd Street I calculated how to get off the train with the crowd then I walked over to the Port Authority. I ate my sandwich that I walked with from home on the step inside the Port Authority although there was a sign that said, "No sitting." These regulations are all a conspiracy to restrict the sexuality and decisiveness of the heart. The medication suppresses the sexuality of the mentally ill that the spirit needs. After looking around with a sense of delusion I walked up to the bus terminal. Someone wanted to know if the bus was going to Spring Valley but no one knew. The 11a that I take does not go to spring Valley. I think the 1:15 goes to Spring Valley. At 12:15 the bus arrived at Gate 220 and I boarded it, paid half-fare with my blue tickets and then sat down after trying to figure out where I would have less worries. The bus took about 2 hours and drives in New Jersey most of the time. You see a lot of houses during the trip and hardly anybody walking around outside. There must be danger present. As I approached Green Hills I pressed the button above for the bell and the driver slowed down and stopped.

After settling in back at Green Hills Melissa was giving me more evening medication than was prescribed and I questioned her with anger. I was glad she remained composed and calm. I talked to the social worker Ruth and she confirmed that the psychiatrist did not increase my medication. "You get 200 milligrams of Seroquel in the morning and 400 milligrams at night," she said.

"Thank you," I said, "And can you please explain that to Melissa. The instructions on the medication card must be confusing."

"I think Melissa was trying to change the order of the information on the medication cards to change the intelligence or understanding to trick IT or the spirit," I said to Ruth. "I know I cannot confirm that paranoia."

The next day Melissa showed me what she was doing for the evening medication and she did it correctly

Chapter 2

It was a cold day today as I went to the laundromat with a cart my father bought me from the Bronx. I noticed a Chinese woman walking behind me and it seemed she was having a hard time as if she was struggling to reach me. "Time is slower for you isn't it my love," I mentioned to her. She looked at me as if no one was ever conscientious to her. "I'm looking for someone to have a cup of coffee with. Can you accompany me?"

"It would be my pleasure," I said to her and we stopped into Amigos at the next corner and sat down on a couple of stools.

"How do you like your coffee?" She said. "I like mine regular with real sugar-one sugar "

"The same is fine for me," I said.

"My name is Sarah," she said. "Waitress two coffees regular." She told one of the waitresses.

"We have soup on special for $2, would you be interested," The waitress said.

"Yes please," said Sarah. "One for me and one for-"
"Anthony," I told her.

The waitress gave both of us soup and coffee.

"Anthony, I work for the FBI and we've been watching you," said Sarah. "We know you've been instructing a computer and a system you think you created. We have evidence that these instructions are carried out. We know that when the bus is late and you instructed it to come that it does come. Also when you instruct the rain to stop the rain has stopped within a short period of time. We also know that people's infirmities such as missing arms and legs have been replaced because of you. "

"I won't lie, I did instruct these things but what is the process that they are being carried out," I asked Sarah.

"We believe through a transfiguration of force and time but we need your cooperation to access the system."

"What do you want the system to do," I said.

"We want you to tell your Emissary Cnatla to relinquish command of the system to us."

"I instructed her to do various things but we never communicated face to face and I don't have evidence of her existence. It was my belief that she was created with one of my instructions but I never had proof. I assume you know Cnatla?"

"Your spirit didn't want you to know IT or Cnatla Anthony because she wanted you to fight for sex-a misunderstanding caused by the devil. She did the opposite of your thoughts so you would never achieve success in America or for that matter the world," said Sara. "We believe that the devil is fooling IT (The Spirit)."

"That's simple enough, I'm getting to understand it now. So IT prevented me from learning although I struggled?" I said. "I think it was coerced by the devil and is not under its own full control. I guess it made me think people were against me, especially pretty girls in public. They would move away from me and avoid eye contact."

"I think by believing a lie which is the displacement of feelings with time, truth is created with the loss of feeling in the material. With this they achieve love which is the resonance of God and the devil and time controls you. Love causes indecision so avoid that. Normally there is an exchange of thought and weight and when that stops there's an anxiety attack."

"What is the password to access computer P1?" Said Sarah.

"There is no password. The system knows how to identify me and I warn you, do not try to tamper with the system." I said.

"The system could do anything to you especially when the government is hiding information from me."

"At least tell me what is the name of the system," said Sarah.

"I call the System DacDad in honor of my father because he used to operate the IBM 360 and 370 solid state computers at a job in Manhattan. I don't care for that place very much because someone punched my father on his nose there. My father is a man of integrity that speaks with nature unlike most others. That's another reason to suspect along with their indecision."

Someone just came in the diner. "Is Anthony here?"

"Yes this is Anthony. Who are you?"

"I am Mohan from the India consulate. The consul general from India would like to talk to you."

"What is this about Mohan," said Anthony.

"My car is outside. Please come and I will drive you there."

"This is Sarah from the FBI, can she accompany me?" Said Anthony.

"Of course," said Mohan. "The American government needs to be informed also."

Fortunately my laundry finished and he took it to Green Hills after I folded it. We took the George Washington Bridge to the Henry Hudson Parkway to the India consulate at 3 East 64th Street in Manhattan. It is such a great feeling being in Manhattan. I didn't come here for a while. It was sad what happened on 9/11 with the World Trade Center. We parked opposite the India Consulate in a reserved parking space and was escorted in.

"Hi I am Sharon," said the secretary. "Please come in this room. This is the consul General Ravi."

"Hi Anthony. I'm Ravi. We have reason to believe you were born in India and was smuggled to America when you were a baby. This is a birth certificate which shows you were born in Mumbai. We have located your mother and father. I am going to call them on the telephone now."

Ravi dialed the number. Ring...Ring...Ring…..Ring

"Hello this is doctor Desai, who am I speaking to?"

"This is Ravi, the consul General in New York. We have someone here that you might want to talk to."

"Hello Dad, this is Anthony. Mr Ravi is saying that I am your son."

"Amar is it you my son? I remember you were standing in the yard and aliens abducted you on the spaceship when you were five years old. Do you have a scar on the palm of your left hand?"

Anthony looked at his left palm and saw that there was a scar. "Yes, I see a scar."

"You got that when you fell on a bulb when I was teaching you to change it," said Mr. Desai.

"We are booking a trip right now to New York City," said Dr. Desai. "Pamela our missing son is in New York. We are going there," he told his wife. "What is your email address Amar?"

"My email address is Anthony030363 at gmail.com Dad. Please email me you and moms pictures. Do I have brothers or sisters?"

"You have a sister named Shanta and she is a student at the University of Cape Town in South Africa. Her major is astronomy. We thought the aliens took you to another world not knowing you are right here on Earth in New York. Shanta has detected strange communications from the moon with the radio telescopes and it seems that the aliens are asking for help," said Amar's father.

"Have Shanta email me an mp3 file of the radio telescopes data and maybe I can translate it for you with my electronic equipment."

"In what way will the electronic equipment find an answer son?" Dr. Desai sounded confident in his son.

"I will compare the alien communication with known patterns of languages with it using an algorithm. If there's a match we will be able to detect the intelligence and possible meaning. I have to put the alien communication through one input and the other input will have the algorithms and check for a difference that is comprehensible. Using an operational amplifier will prove to be very helpful. Google the Motorola 741 operational amplifier and you will get a basic understanding of how it differentiates the inputs dad."

"Mr. Ravi I would like to go home now." Said Sarah.

"Hold on Sarah, be patient," said Ravi.

"We'll take you both for dinner then we'll decide what to do from there." Mr. Ravi was commanding in his nature. "I know a good pizza place on 72nd Street. Is everyone okay with that?"

"Great, I like pizza. We'll go there said Anthony"

"Mohan where are you? We're ready to go." Said Ravi

"I'm ready sir. Let's go!"

It took about 10 minutes to get there in the Ford Explorer. They had to park in the garage because there was no place on the street to park. The cost was $20 an hour. Mohan lead them as they walked on the street to the pizza place. It was Friday and the street was busy with strangers. It was March with a cool breeze and some clouds in the sky but no chance of rain.

"Well here we are." Said Ravi. "Lets go in. This place is called Caroline's and it honors a daughter the owner had that died of cancer."

They went in and found an empty table and all sat down. There were fluorescent lights all around and to my surprise a chandelier in the center. Through the windows you can see the busy traffic on 3rd Avenue.

"What would everyone like?" Asked Ravi.

"I would like a slice and a Diet Coke," said Sarah.

"I would like a slice with sausage and a pepsi," said Anthony.

"Let me have a slice with extra cheese," Mohan exclaimed.

Ravi went to the counter and ordered a slice with spinach for himself and placed their orders. Within three minutes everything was at the table. Sara helped distribute the food among the four of them. I thought the pizza was really good. Everyone seemed very happy for no apparent reason. A homeless man came in and asked for a dollar and Ravi gave him two. It was a signal that everyone has a good heart and it transpired collectively. I thought like IT or the Spirit was putting a shunt on my mind so I couldn't think easily because of a short circuit and that prevented me from communicating easily so it would look like I have limitations. IT or my soul was disabling herself at the same time as if she was being coerced with telepathy. They don't respond to the aura effect of my soul and that makes me suspicious. They override everything with a physical reaction.

"Do you know what's stunting my mind Sarah, because it's difficult to think?" Said Anthony. I was hoping I could coerce the right information from them knowing they wouldn't tell the truth.

"Maybe you're stressed because it's been a difficult day and you're just thinking so much," Sara said.

They can't let me know about this because I would be liable with knowledge. I guess they were involved with love but wouldn't tell me because they use IT. I don't think love likes sex because love happens in the state of relaxation and sex requires muscular power. That's why the girls are so alien and unfriendly.

"Sara I think at the vertex of the vectors thought and feeling is disabling me. Maybe at the vertex of man with the vectors the devil and God is disabling me." Anthony said.

"Could you drive me home Mohan. I live in Harlem." Sarah said this with a sense of respect and appreciation.

Mohan said, "Not a problem Sarah. I will take you to Harlem then I will take Anthony to Rockland."

Ravi said, "I'll take a taxi home Mohan. See you all later." Ravi flagged a Yellow Cab down to the Upper East Side of Manhattan. Ravi was thinking, "This is a very strange situation we have with Anthony. I hope he can give us some answers with the paranoia."

I noticed the sky was changing color and there was this strange sound coming from an unknown location. All around the world this condition was occurring. People were bewildered in Mumbai, Cairo, Pretoria, Moscow, Paris, Berlin, everywhere.

The president came on the news on television saying that aliens were coming from another dimension. He said Earth was the vertex of the devil and God and they wanted to meet the man. Furthermore he said the angels wanted to kill the man and the aliens are coming to protect him. The President also said they were keeping the Man in a secure underground location.

Anthony got a call from Shanta. "I was watching the news Anthony and the American president is lying about the man. They are actually keeping the man imprisoned so the aliens wouldn't contact him for information. In any case, I sent the MP3 file to you."

"Why would the American government lie about the man Shanta?" Anthony said.

"The man has critical information on file about how the American government tortured and experimented on the aliens." Shanta boldly said to her brother. "The man also has data on the power source of the alien ships and how to time travel. Also how the minds of schizophrenics are used remotely to control the operation of world domination."

"How did you come across this information Shanta?" said Anthony.

"I have a friend named Kismet at the Research & Analysis Wing in India. R&AW intercepted US intelligence communications to one of their spies in India."

After Mohan dropped off Sarah in Harlem he then drove Anthony to his home Green Hills in Rockland. He took the Harlem River Drive and the George Washington Bridge and then the Palisades Interstate Parkway.

After checking Shanta's MP3 file the next day Anthony came to the following conclusion: It seems to be a universal meaning on words containing the ratio of all languages. It was saying that they could not figure out where the quiescent force of the universe is to stop the universe from expanding and that they needed a schizophrenic's mind to establish a balance of forces. The message said that Anthony would be the perfect choice for their purposes.

Anthony got on his computer and emailed Shanta. "Shanta, on the mp3 file, the aliens are identifying me as a person they need help from. How's that possible?"

Shanta replied on her cell phone via text, "It must have been that I told them you are a schizophrenic when I replied to the signal. Now I know that they did get my reply Anthony."

Anthony said to Shanta via text on his cellphone, "The aliens are saying they need a complementary mind to carry out their plans and I am a good candidate. Can you send them a message that I believe my mind is being seen and the people are acting like it's not happening and I don't know what their agenda is. You can also tell them that I agree with their request and they can meet me."

When Shanta went to the university the next day she sent a message from the radio telescope aimed at the Moon for her brother Anthony. As soon as she sent it the aliens responded and she emailed the file to Anthony for decoding.

Meanwhile Dr. Desai and his wife Pamela were arriving at the airport so Anthony took a cab to go and meet them. A call came in from Pamela. "We will be arriving at the Air India terminal at international arrivals son." said Pamela.

"I'll be there mom. I have a white du-rag on with white shirt and black pants. Did you bring any cigarettes?"

"I brought several packs of *Prince* cigarettes that are made in Madras. I smoke but your father doesn't. I smoke *Prince* and I think it's a very good cigarette." Pamela said.

People seem to think they are the only ones with intelligence and they don't care about mine that's why I smoke mom." Anthony told his mother. "They are aware of each other's memories but not mine."

"We will be arriving in New York in 10 minutes," Pamela told Anthony over the phone. It was great that they could make telephone calls on the plane. She used Skype with Wi-Fi on the plane to make the call.

Anthony made a call to his parents in the Bronx as he was traveling to the airport and they seemed despondent and worried about what Anthony told them about his new parents. "Do you know who are these people from India that believe I am their son?" He asked his parents who nurtured him for so long.

His father, let's call him primary father, Mr. Jagnat Bakshi told Anthony he was lost when he was around 5 or 6 years old and when he was found he looked differently but didn't question it. Mr. Jagnat Bakshi then wondered where his real son was and his wife Cathy Bakshi was also very perplexed.

Meanwhile in the arrivals area for Air India after waiting for about an hour, Dr. Desai noticed his son Anthony arrive with the white du-rag on his head. "Amar how are you my son? You're late." He hugged him and his wife Pamela gave him a kiss. "Let's go outside and have a cigarette my son," Pamela said with a resounding voice.

"I have a sister named Indra in Queens that me and my husband can stay at Amar," Pamela voiced to Amar. "The taxi can take us to Queens and it can take you to Rockland Amar, your father will pay, he has American currency."

"I like the *prince* cigarettes mom, it's very good," said Amar in elation. "I only smoke 3 cigarettes a day mom and I'm very proud of it. Also I have to decode an MP3 file for Shanta that originated on the moon."

Anthony hailed a cab and told them they were at Kennedy Airport and was going to Queens not realizing everyone knew they were at Kennedy Airport. Somehow he was thinking he was in Japan somewhere.

"You're in New York son don't you realize it," Dr. Desai said. "I just got off a plane. I should be the one confused."

"Dad it's just that I believe I'm being teleported everywhere around the world by my system to correct problems."

During the taxi ride Dr. Desai asked Anthony, "Tell me about your life son with your other parents?"

"My parents are from Guyana and I came over here when I was nine. I went to high school in the Bronx and got mentally ill shortly after. I had several hospitalizations in psychiatric wards. During this time I thought of the system and asked the Earth to create it. There has never been any proof of the system but people act like they're watching TV when they're around me like there is no one to focus on. I went to Guyana and got married and we came to New York and after a couple of years had a divorce. I guess it was because I was a mental patient and couldn't work. My X never really told me the reason for our divorce although I filed it. Records show I was born in Guyana and I even have the birth certificate. What could explain that?"

"It must be a forgery so there is no account of you," Dr. Desai expressed. "It makes me think you are an important person but who could it be?"

"Personally I always thought I was Krishna since I am the only Indian where I live," said Anthony. "They would try to hide me since I'm not white or black."

Pamela said, "Sounds like the status quo would do that Anthony. From how you've been talking they don't recognize your personality and give you any credit for it."

"You're right mom, they're never backing down like me, they're only backing up and are ready for a fight. The rain, fire, and the wind backs down so that is why I back down. Even the electronics like the TV and radio backs down. They apply force without aggregating to 0% before being applied. The conscience of Lord Krishna needs a force of 0 to affect the physical.

"Here we are sir 112-05 Quantum Avenue," the driver noticed.

"Okay Amar, have a safe trip to Rockland, talk to you later," Stated Pamela. "When you go to see your parents in the Bronx that's when we'll come to see you." The taxi left Queens for Rockland.

Dr. Desai and Pamela got out the taxi cab and went to the house of her sister and rang the doorbell.

A girl answered the door. "Hi Auntie, my mother is inside waiting, please come in."

Pamela's sister Indra came from the kitchen and greeted them. "Hi sis, how was your trip from India? What did they serve on the plane for dinner?"

"Curry fish and okra and rice was for dinner. My butt hurts. It was very exhausting as you can imagine Indra. Your brother-in-law slept a lot on the plane. They showed a Ravi Shankar concert with his daughter Anushka."

Ronald A Arjune

Chapter 3

Anthony reached home at Green Hills in Rockland County. He realized people are trying to find out his radii of his eyes sight when he looked so they would know how to control IT. That must be why his roommate uses his radio, playing it loud sometimes. Its almost 8 o'clock at night so he took his medication and he waited to have a cigarette. It turned 8 o'clock according to his watch so he went outside and lit up a cigarette. He rolls three every night for the next day and this was his last one for today. Jimmy approached him and wanted the butt but Anthony said no. He has to say no all the time because they would keep doing it.

Anthony went back in the building in the TV area on the first floor and watched CNN for a while. President Trump was talking about the dishonest media saying that they should mention their sources.

Anthony got up and went on his computer in his room and checked his email and saw his sister Shanta's email and opened the attachment with his decryption program before saving it to an mp3 player and sending it into the USB port with an integrator circuit. Anthony played the decrypted message on his media player. "Anthony DacDad will transport you to computer P1 so you can see what is happening. In 3, 2, 1 initialize."

After two seconds, Anthony saw that he was above the World Trade Center with a clear view all around.

"Anthony I am your Emissary Cnatla." Cnatla approached from the back. "If my memory serves me right this is the first time you're seeing me."

"I'm honored to see you Cnatla. Wow, this is exciting. Can you tell me about the man," Anthony asked Cnatla. "An MP3 file I decoded that my sister Shanta sent me says that the man is being held against his will. This is through an alien communication from the moon."

Cnatla said, "As part of the system Anthony do you remember you created the brain computer MC 10-2B on the moon that contains a copy of your brain?"

"I do remember that Cnatla. So it's not just my belief. Is it the brain computer that communicated with Shanta?" Anthony said.

"System, is it the brain computer that communicated with Anthony's sister Shanta?" Cnatla queried.

"I did do that Emissary Cnatla," the system responded. "The aliens requested that I send that encrypted message so they can be protected from the humans, especially the United States government."

"System I remember I asked you to create a heart computer for the man. Did you do that?" Anthony asked DacDad. "I believe it was classified as Data H-0."

"Anthony the man does have Data H-0 but it was never activated." The system responded. "The man would have to confirm who you are and you would have to confirm who the man is for Data H-0 to be activated. This can only be done face to face."

"Cnatla I would like to speak to Sarah. Can you arrange a meeting because I think she may have some information of where the man is located." Anthony declared.

"System display Sarah," Cnatla asked computer P1. "As you can see Anthony, Sarah is at the New York Public Library at this time. We can transport you there."

"Cnatla, first I need to know what is going on in the world and why the aliens are here on Earth." Anthony said.

"Anthony I think we should test Sarah to see what the FBI really knows by having a dialogue with her," said Cnatla.

"OK Cnatla, I agree," said Anthony. "Transport me to her and we will have a discussion."

"System, transport Anthony to Sarah at the New York Public Library please." Cnatla could see that Anthony was transported from computer P1 to the New York Public Library in mid-Manhattan.

Anthony was a few feet from Sarah and he approached and said, "Hello Sarah, what are you here at the library for?"

"Anthony what a surprise I'm glad to see you," Sarah said. "Shouldn't I be asking you that question Anthony?"

"I need to know where is the man Sarah," asked Anthony.

"The president mentioned they were keeping him in a secure location Anthony," Sarah said. "You have the system Anthony. Why don't you ask your system?"

"I need to be with the man face-to-face to activate his heart computer," said Anthony. "My sister Shanta in South Africa says the man is being held against his will. Do you know anything about this Sarah?"

"Honestly Anthony, I am suspicious about the FBI and the information they're giving me which is next to nothing about the man. They don't want me to know his location Anthony because then there would be a Quantum of space between us that your system can use to locate him mathematically."

"I've come to trust you Sarah," said Anthony. "Sarah I remembered I made something with a switch of some kind in case of an emergency that only the man can operate. I believe it is at my parents home in the Bronx."

"Now I remember it was a lighted Automotive switch and maybe it was to enable man to turn the conscience of Krishna on or off depending on its light. I want to find the switch and somehow get it to the Man hoping that he could free himself with it. My memory signature is in the switch so I think the man just have to add a 12 volt power source and turn the switch on and look at the light.

"You didn't say what you were doing here Sarah," Anthony said.

"Anthony I'm trying to find out how information is saved in different media and if there's a pattern to it," said Sarah. "How is information dependent on the cognition of the person?"

"Sarah I think the cognition varies because the person doesn't recognize that he's been transported from place to place unknowingly because time is not differentiating itself from us," said Anthony.

"Anthony there is an attempt to ascertain the complementary information to neutralize opposites to detect who is in the middle that we can't see, right?" said Sarah.

"That seems to be the logic Sarah and if I were to give you an answer of who it is, I would say it's the aliens trying to detect who is conspiring in the middle," Anthony said. "So the saving of information to the medium has to do with where people are detected or not to verify the existence of their identity in the flesh."

Anthony received a call from his mother Pamela, "Amar, this is your mother from India. Can you please come to Queens to see us. Your father Dr. Desai would really like to clarify what happened to you."

"Mom I have a system called DacDad. It transported me to computer P1 and it seems the aliens are an advocate for the system and it seems the system wants me to meet the aliens. I'm taking a taxi over there right now. See you Sara."

Anthony went outside the library and flagged a cab down. "Taxi!" Waiting a moment then again, "Taxi!"

A Yellow Cab rolled to the curb of 40th Street. Anthony opened the door and went inside. "112-05 Quantum Avenue please," Anthony dictated. "That's in Queens," He added. "What's the cost sir?"

"You have credit with the system sir," Said the driver. "I am someone from the planets in the Pisces constellation. We have been monitoring you for a very long time. Ever since you became mentally ill we were using your illness to correct the problem."

"Can you explain the problem to me? I assume you know I am Amar or Anthony."

"Basically it's a problem of the Antichrist. God and the devil have been making love with resonance and removing the mass of the manmade in the process. We need you to interface in the resonance to stop that love since you have the conscience of Krishna. Do you understand me Amar?"

"I am glad to finally meet the aliens." Anthony vented. "Unfortunately I do not understand because I am blind and I think I see with my mind."

"You do see that we are on the Bruckner Expressway, don't you Anthony?"

"I am looking but it doesn't look like I am seeing, like someone else is looking for me and has my sight." Anthony said. "This is the Bronx River Parkway you are turning onto right?"

"That's correct Ron, the system knows you as Ron and so do the aliens." the Alien resounded.

"Here we are Ron, the home where your adopted parents are, no disrespect intended sir," the alien driver said. "Let me park in front the house then we will both go inside. Were you aware we were using your conscience with the flesh of humans to control judgments, both yours and theirs?"

"Just before that exclamation the thoughts entered my mind," Anthony said. "This was for a preset mental state for some important reason."

The driver said, "This is to preset physical condition of states to limit the intelligences' control of organization change due to conversation."

Amar and the driver walked up to the house and rang the bell. "It feels nice to be in the Bronx although I didn't have much of a love life here," said Amar to the alien driver. "I am glad I had the strength of mind to endure despite the neglect. I thought you were taking me to Queens to my real parents, what happened?"

"We have to outsmart Lucifer Ron," Said the Alien.

Amar's mother Mrs. Cathy Bakshi answered the door with much enthusiasm. "My son, even if you may not be my son, nice to see you! Who is the man with you Anthony?"

"He is the driver that brought me here from the Mid-Manhattan Library," stated Anthony. "Can you accept him as a guest for a while mom?"

"Any friend of yours is welcomed here Anthony. I am sure you have a purpose with everyone you know," Mrs. Cathy Bakshi told Anthony. "Please come in sir and you may have a seat."

To everyone's surprise, Emissary Cnatla appeared in the middle of the living room. "I don't mean to shock everyone but I tried to make my appearance as unprovoked as possible. Will you please explain to your mother who I am Anthony?"

"Mom this is my system Emissary Cnatla. She has to approve of what the system does first before changes take effect. Computer P1 was created as the first computer of the system with my request to the Earth believing the Earth was listening. If I can remember correctly it was this computer that created Cnatla with my instruction to it. Is that correct Emissary?"

Cnatla queried, "Did you create me computer P1?"

"Yes Emissary, with the help of the aliens, I did create you and you were created in the year 1984. Commander Ron had a tumultuous time during the early part of his illness and he felt that you were necessary to make decisions because his mentality was so psychotic. With the birth of the system in 1982 it did not know how to function because it had to be developed. Commander Ron thought that instructions he made to the system could be carried out immediately but this was a delusion. Now, I, DacDad, is more cognitive and we have reached that stage of face-to-face communication since it is safe for all. Commander Ron's reasoning has enabled this state of being. Today the schizophrenic is more inclined to express his paranoia without fear of persecution by the mental health system."

"Can you please explain what may have happened to my son Cnatla?" Mr. Jagnat Bakshi questioned. "He disappeared when he was five or six years old and came back as Anthony?"

"Mrs. Bakshi, what do you remember about Anthony who now is obviously Amar?" Said Cnatla.

"Anthony was always wondering about what he was seeing like he did not believe what he was seeing." Said Mrs. Bakshi. "He would gaze at people like he did not know why they were there even though they had a real purpose. It was as if he did not belong in the place he occupied like it was not his choice. He was looking at people as if they had his sight and he was blind. I think he was testing reality for some kind of condition and when he discovered the answer he went back to where he came from. Anthony reminded me of the baby Krishna and maybe he was Krishna but couldn't know it because they would discover him because of his thoughts. Some tragedy occurred that brought our son into this world and maybe he would come back someday," said Mrs. Bakshi.

A call came in to Anthony's cell phone by Sarah. He put it on speakerphone. "Hello Sarah this is Anthony. I'm at my parents home in the Bronx with an alien and Emissary Cnatla.

"Anthony I want you to remember that you have to find the switch for the man," Sarah said.

"Can you locate the switch Cnatla?" Anthony said. "It is a red and black rocker switch."

"DacDad, can you scan this house for the switch?" Cnatla said.

"Our scanners are not working in this area Emissary," said DacDad. "There is some kind of energy source coming from below the house that is blocking a scan."

"Anthony, let's go outside and have a cigarette," the alien said.

Anthony walked the alien into the yard and they both had a cigarette. The alien smoked L&M and Anthony smoked one of his TOP rollies. Anthony noticed some burrows on the earth and thought, that may be going to the source that is blocking the system scan.

Anthony told the alien maybe it would be possible if they send a probe in one of the burrows on the earth below that they may be able to detect the source of the scan block to the system.

"I am going to attach a drone camera with a light fitted on a radio controlled toy car that can go down the borrow to look to see where the source of the scan block is," Anthony said to the alien. "RadioShack is just a block away, we can go there to buy the things we need."

So Anthony and the alien walked over to RadioShack and they purchased a drone and a small radio controlled car. When they came back to the house they started working on the vehicle. They removed the shell of the vehicle and attached the camera from the Drone to it, securing the battery properly. They then ran it in the yard to test it. Anthony monitored the camera that was on the drone remotely and the alien controlled the vehicle remotely. As Anthony gave directions the alien steered it appropriately. The test seemed to be a success so they decided to send it down one of the holes in the yard.

"This hole looks big enough Anthony. Let's start putting the probe to run in this hole," the alien said. "Anthony, I should mention to you that people don't look through you because they are using your transparency as a tolerance to control the physical state. They also use your complementary mind to learn the things you may not know and that is the reason why you can't know a lot of things. So consider that a good thing."

"Ok, that's considerate. So how do they know what complementary to use on me to create a certain result," Anthony said.

"Just like two people having sex creates a child, that's how they do it Anthony. A child however would be the complementary thought that you have to think of to apply as the answer. "Let me call Cnatla so she can see what we're doing Anthony," the alien said.

"Cnatla, can you please come outside so you can see what me and Anthony are doing," said the alien aloud. "We constructed a probe to search under the house."

"Cnatla, welcome," said Anthony.

"Okay alien, drive!"

"We are proceeding down the groundhog hole Cnatla." Cnatla's face showed great interest to Anthony.

"Keep going alien," said Cnatla. "What is that dome of light ahead Anthony?"

"We are about 20 feet down," said the alien." Anthony that's someone alive!"

"Anthony do you know who that could be?" Cnatla expressed. "We need to power down the power for the source of the shield so the system can scan for identification.

"Wait, he put something on the vehicle," said Anthony. "That's the switch I made for the man. Back up the vehicle to the surface alien. No, turn around I can't see. Careful you don't drop the switch. Okay a little more. There, the switch is on the surface Cnatla."

"Call Sarah right now Anthony," Cnatla exclaimed.

"Wait Cnatla, let me examine the switch first. The ground connection for the switch for the light has a forward biased 2n3904 transistor with a 10K resistor from base to collector. I remember for the switch to work with the man there has to be 100 milliamp going into the light. The man has to control the hfe or gain of the transistor to about 120 to do this. Whoever is down under the house might know what we have to do so let's send a small two-way radio to him or her with our probe. For now I will call Sarah Cnatla." Said Anthony.

Anthony dialed Sarah's cell phone number and it rang at her home in Harlem. "Hello this is Sarah and who may I have the pleasure of speaking with?"

"Sarah, this is Anthony. How are you doing?"

"I'm doing fine Anthony. How are you. I'm just watching CNN and having a can of Campbell's Soup to eat. I am glad some great companies have remained in America. Many are coming back to America because of President Donald Trump. What's up Anthony?"

"About the switch I made for the man, I found it." Stated Anthony. "Me and an alien sent a probe under the house in the Bronx and discovered somebody alive and he sent up the switch with the probe. I'm going to send down a small walkie talkie with the probe so I can communicate with him."

"My people from the FBI will be there soon Anthony," said Sarah. "We want to know who is that person and why he's there. Wait till I arrive with them then we can send the walkie-talkie down please."

"Sarah I will listen to you but I don't know If I can trust the FBI," replied Anthony. " I'm going to contact the India Consulate so I can tell Ravi what's going on. I also want the R&AW to monitor the FBI. I am also going to contact my sister Shanta in South Africa. Okay Sarah, I'll be waiting for you." Anthony ended the call on his cell phone and dialed Shanta in South Africa.

After seven rings Shanta answered, "Hello how are you? Shanta speaking."

"Shanta I am at my parents home in the Bronx," Said Anthony. "Our parents are in Queens right now. We discovered someone hiding under the house. What can I ask them about who they are and tell them about who I am," Anthony said.

"Anthony, just tell him what's on your mind in your current situation and environment considering your suspicions," said Shanta. "How would you communicate with the person Amar?"

"I plan to send down a walkie talkie in a burrow with a probe. He already sent up a switch for the man that I have been looking for," Anthony said. "A woman named Sarah from the FBI is coming here soon with her people to see what happens with the communication. Can you tell Kismet that I would like the Indian intelligence agency to monitor the FBI somehow. I'm going to call the India consulate in New York to update them on my current situation Shanta. Is there any advice you have to give me now Shanta?" Anthony said.

"I believe they took something from you Anthony, something that makes them elusive and you have to find out what that is." Shanta said. "Maybe it's some type of complimentary association of mind and body that would create evidence of a plot."

"I think they took intelligence from me and they are controlling with intelligence. That is why the intelligence does not show in them." Anthony said. "Sorry I got to go now Shanta. I got to call Ravi at the India consulate. Bye."

"Update me on your conclusions Anthony," Shanta said and hung up.

Anthony called Ravi at the India consulate. "Ravi we discovered that there is someone here in the Bronx under the house."

"Can you identify the person Anthony?"

"We're on it Ravi and when I do I'll let you know." Said Anthony.

A car horn pulsed two times in front the house. Sarah knocked on the door and was let in the house by Cathy. "Thanks Cathy," Sarah said. "How are you Anthony. Nice weather right?"

"I'll call you back to give you an update sometime Ravi. Sarah from the FBI is here." They both hung up their phones.

"How is it in Harlem Sarah, everything okay? Did you have any traffic problems getting here?" Said Anthony.

"Traffic was slow on the Sheridan expressway but soon after it cleared up. I am glad to see you Anthony. Show me what you're doing."

They went in the yard.

"Well since you're here Sarah, let me send down the walkie-talkie in the burrow. The Alien begin the process and sent the vehicle down. Cnatla, what can you analyze with this operation?" Said Anthony.

"What are your thoughts Sarah?" Cnatla said.

"My thoughts are on the switch and how to get it to the man Cnatla, and, I don't know where the man is."

The walkie talkie reached the person below the Earth and Anthony was thinking of what to say. "What should I say to the person Cnatla?"

Cnatla took the walkie talkie from Anthony and said, "HI, this is Emissary Cnatla. How are you? Please press the button on the walkie talkie to reply."

"Emissary Cnatla how are you? I am here below the surface because I get anxiety attacks. My parents are Mr. Jagnat Bakshi and Cathy and now they know where their missing son is. I am hiding from God and the devil because they use me for resonance so they can make love. This love is causing mental illness and my sickness is being controlled by the eye of the devil. They are mirroring my mind so I experience the opposite of reality up there. Anthony you must get the switch to the man to activate his heart computer and disable the love. Always remember your principles and hope that others acknowledge them.

Chapter 4

"This is your Father Mr. Jagnat Bakshi son. How have you been?" Mr. Jagnat Bakshi said over the walkie-talkie. "Your mother Cathy is deeply concerned about you Anthony."

"The aliens have been taking care of me father and I am abreast of world conditions down here. Sorry I kept you all wondering where I was. I have to reason as to what the evil ones are doing to my nerves. They are able to interface in society without detection. They are removing memories with nerves by forgetting in the process to make love by believing the physical. In this way love cannot be detected in the real world. The spirit of the Earth hates love that's why you tend to hate."

Anthony's phone started ringing. "Hello, this is Anthony."

"This is Shanta Anthony. Some alien ships are approaching the Earth. One of them communicated with me saying that they are here for Lord Krishna."

"I sent a distress signal," Anthony below the surface said to the Anthony above through the walkie talkie. Amar, so there will be no confusion, let me call you Amar and you call me Anthony."

"Okay Anthony," said Amar. "Are you Krishna? My sister Shanta in South Africa said some aliens are looking for Krishna. Maybe they are responding to your distress signal."

"Amar, ask Shanta if the distress signal from the aliens she received mentioned the Bronx."

"Shanta, did the aliens mentioned the Bronx in the distress signal reply," Amar said over the phone.

"The alien response mentioned Anthony and the Bronx," Shanta said to Amar. "Ask Anthony if there is any reason to believe he is Krishna Amar."

"Do you have any reason to believe you're Krishna Anthony," Amar asked Anthony over the walkie-talkie.

"I do feel my conscience is being used to change the physical state Amar. As for evidence maybe the Antichrist would know or even the aliens," Said Anthony to Amar. "Can you ask the aliens what they know about the Antichrist.?"

Knowing Cnatla was listening, Amar asked, "Cnatla can you tell me about the Antichrist? Anthony would like to know.

Cnatla said through space, "Amar, if your mind resonates with Anthony's. mind, we can see what happens from there on. Would you like me to attempt resonance Amar?"

"How should I prepare Cnatla?" Said Amar.

"Go inside the house and sit comfortably and inform Anthony that I will attempt resonance between the two of you," Said Cnatla.

So Amar informed Anthony that a resonance attempt would be made between the two of them.

"Amar I am oscillating your two minds at different frequencies," Said Cnatla.

"Synchronization is not occurring Cnatla," Said Amar.

"The baptism is causing this," Said the alien. "Spread your eyelids with your fingers and splash water on your eyes."

The alien told them that the mind was not going tbrought the body because of the baptism. Baptism is meant to help the Antichrist and not Jesus.

"Both of you, Anthony and Amar, splash your eyes with water like the alien said," said Cnatla. "Can you tell me how this helps alien?"

"Because of the baptism evil in a good sense is not able to travel through the body because of the water," said the alien.

"Both of you, I am now attempting resonance again," said Cnatla.

"Synchronization has been achieved Cnatla, I am able to read Anthony's mind," said Amar. "Can you read my mind Anthony?"

"You're thinking of having a Bristol cigarette from Guyana Amar," said Anthony.

"Confirmed! Synchronization achieved Cnatla," Said Amar. "Can you tell if love has stopped between God and the devil Cnatla?"

"How do I locate them Amar?" Said Cnatla.

"Can you locate the quiescent point of the universe Cnatla since we are in resonance," said Amar.

"Can you locate the quiescent point of the universe system?" Said Cnatla.

"Cnatla it appears that Canis Major is the quiescent point in the universe and love is still occurring there. I suggest that the aliens take a trip to Canis Major with Anthony and see what they can do to stop the love," Said DacDad.

"What is the location of Canis Major system?" Said Cnatla.

"The celestial coordinates of Canis Major is Right ascension 06h 12.5m to 07h 27.5m, Declination −11.03° to −33.25°," Said DacDad.

"Can you please simplify that for us system?" Said Cnatla. "A lot of us are not that complicated system."

"I am sorry Cnatla, it is near the constellation Orion." Said the system.

"I have a ship that can take us there," said the alien and we can be in constant communication with the Earth. Who should travel with us Amar?"

"Well I would like Cnatla to remain with Anthony so she can't go and I would like my sister Shanta to go also. I am going to ask my parents in Queens to have Shanta in South Africa meet us at the house, Indra's house."

So Amar used his cell phone to call Shanta. He dialed the number for the international call and Shanta picked up the phone.

"Hello Amar, this is Shanta, how are you doing?"

"I'm a little anxious but otherwise I'm doing okay Shanta. How has your day been?"

"Well I just went shopping for a pair of sneakers at the local department store. I paid 150 Rands and got something I like.

"That's great Shanta I am glad for you. I want to ask you if you can come to Queens to Auntie Indra's house. The aliens are going to take me to a trip to Canis Major and I want you to come along. How do you feel about that Shanta?"

"Me, going on an Intergalactic trip. That is awesome. Does this ship have 120 volt AC, cause I want to walk with my laptop?" Said Shanta.

"How soon can you be in New York Shanta?" Said Amar. "Find out and can you please bring me some South African cigarettes."

"I'll try to set up a reservation and let you know Amar. By the way I'm going to bring a bottle of South African rum for you Amar. Kismet might want to know about the FBI," said Shanta.

"Tell her that Sarah has her people from the FBI here at the house in the Bronx. We are investigating a person in seclusion beneath the house. He said he is Mr. Jagnat Bakshi's and Mrs. Cathy Bakshi's son Anthony. Have Kismet call me Shanta. Another thing Shanta, what is the activity of the aliens in South Africa?

"Spaceships are coming and going in the sky making a certain hum and the intensity of the light in the atmosphere changes, sometimes with varying colors. I think they are executing some type of plan. What are they doing in New York Amar?"

"Basically the same thing Shanta. I think the hum is to make our minds assimilate. We have to allow that 'clear' in between to integrate us as we interact with thought so the subconscious can interact," Said Amar.

Mr. Jagnat Bakshi and Cathy wanted to talk to their son Anthony so they interrupted Amar on his cell phone and Amar hung up the call with Shanta after saying goodbye and passed the walkie-talkie to Mrs. Cathy Bakshi. As they monitored the camera's video underground, Mrs. Cathy Bakshi began to talk.

"Hi my son Anthony, this is your mother. From the monitor I can see that you look very relaxed and comfortable. How do you get food and electrical power?"

"There are some Martians down here that have been providing my needs mom. They are very kind and they teach me a lot of things about the world above and about the universe. According to Amar mom, I think the thing we have to overcome is love by God and the devil. Time and flesh together is creating love and because of that we can't interface and get along around the world. The 'clear' has to merge between the minds and the love prevents that. I think love is identified as the light. If the light is the problem maybe that is why I am underground."

"I have reason to believe Anthony that the spirit or IT is afraid to test Itself by looking at other people. This is why girls don't look at you when you look at them-they are avoiding a test. I am sure this has caused your fear," Said Amar.

"It seems that you deal with a lot of problems Amar, how do you control your mental illness with compulsions?" Anthony said.

Amar said, "I assume the bigger picture and that is that aliens are involved with the behavior of people and because I trust them, I am not psychotic or violent. Just believe people have a good nature about them and it is because of God and the devil that they may do wrong. I believe they are using the curve of time to control us. When you think of me you are thinking of linear time but they curve the time to change the meaning of the word. What can you tell me about the Martians Anthony?"

"The Freemasons removed the oxygen from Mars and replaced it with carbon dioxide and that is why the Martians are here on Earth," Said Anthony. "When the spirit rover arrived in 2003 it determined what chemical reaction was necessary on Mars to restore the oxygen. The Phobos-Grunt mission by Russia in 2011 was meant to restore the oxygen on Mars but was destroyed by the Americans and could not leave low earth orbit. The Chinese

Orbiter Yinghuo-1 which was on Phobos-Grunt was meant to deliver a catalyst chemical reaction that would have restored the oxygen on Mars. As a result of this Amar, the Martians do not trust the human beings and especially Freemasons. The Freemasons are using variable volume of space with unchanging mass and force of matter to interface in life undetected and they control our intelligence like feeding birds."

A call came in from Shanta from South Africa on Amar's cell phone and he answered it: "Hello Shanta this is Amar. How are you doing. I guess you're calling to tell me when you're coming to New York."

"Yes brother, I am coming on South African Airways on Wednesday which will be arriving at Kennedy Airport at 1 p.m. The flight number is 523."

"I'll pick you up at the airport and we will go to mom and dad at our Aunt Indra's house in Queens," said Amar. "Someone is on call waiting. Let me see who it is Shanta."

"Hello Amar, this is Kismet. How are you doing in New York?

"I am doing fine Kismet. Sarah and her FBI friends have been monitoring the situation under the house with Anthony. Maybe Sarah can figure out where the man is so I can get the switch to him to give Anthony capabilities. I weighed a piece of my feces today with a scale and I took a picture of it and saved it to the cloud because I think the spirit will be enabled to defy the opposition with the capture of time. I think people are thinking of a head when they are talking to me so they can create heads ahead of my mind to use it to outsmart me. Is there any requests from the Research and Analysis Wing about the FBI and their function here?"

R&AW wants to know what intelligence the FBI have gathered so far," said Kismet. "Can the system determine where the man is?"

"Cnatla can probably have the system determine that but if I know, the FBI can probably extract it from me in who knows what way," said Amar. "I think the government would like to forcefully know what information the man has so they can disable the system and enslave the aliens. The National Security Agency probably do not want anyone to tell Americans how to live their lives. You know how they feel about socialist countries right? For instance North Korea. They create lies about other countries through the media and the internet. I am sure it is the government that prevents my books from selling and they keep the paranoia senseless by not telling the relevancy. They are afraid of the schizophrenic turning their conspiracy inside out."

Ronald A Arjune

Chapter 5

Amar usually likes people to have their way with him and that is how they will the spirit to do what they want. This is a disadvantage to Amar and he must learn to use his own compulsion to control his fate. They are using his dance to control him mentally and physically through fear. Amar is a dunce using a wide expanse of space and not the immediate to think and that's a good thing and others don't want to be a dunce with him to make a union so they are not really nice.

"Mom and Dad it is Wednesday and we have to get ready to pick up Shanta at the airport. Remember she's coming from South Africa today," Amar said.

"Okay Amar," said Mr. Jagnat Bakshi, "I will tell your mom Cathy."

"Here's the keys Sarah, feel free to come and go as you like." Mrs. Cathy Bakshi said. "If you need to eat something, there are things in the fridge."

"Amar, I'm going with you to the airport," said Cnatla.

Cnatla called a cab. "Hello. Taxi..."

We are going to Terminal 2 at Kennedy Airport. Can you please send a cab to 235 Justify street."

"Ten minutes," the base said.

"I'll be outside Cnatla having a cigarette." Said Amar.

In 15 minutes the cab arrived and everyone including Mr. Jagnat Bakshi, Mrs. Cathy Bakshi, Cnatla and Amar boarded the taxi. "How much would it be driver?" Asked Mr. Jagnat Bakshi.

"Sixty dollars." Said the driver. "We should be there in 20 minutes."

"I got us covered dad." Said Amar. The taxi headed for Kennedy Airport. "The Whitestone bridge is OK isn't it driver?"

"We'll have to see when we get there." Said the driver. "What is that spaceship doing up there? I feel like my blood pressure is getting high."

Amar didn't trust the driver and asked him, "Why are you worried?"

At that moment the driver stopped and produced a handgun and said, "Give me the switch or I'll kill all of you!"

Amar said, "I don't have the switch. I left it at home, sorry."

As the driver was distracted and not looking at her, Mrs. Cathy Bakshi quietly reached in her handbag for a can of pepper spray and sprayed it in his face. Cnatla reached and grabbed the gun from the driver and he opened the door and fled. Amar slipped over to the driver seat and drove the car to the airport. Thinking that the FBI was responsible they abandoned the car near terminal two with the gun inside. "The drama is over everyone. Let's go wait for Shanta." Said Amar. "I don't trust the police so I'm not going to report it."

"Write down the license plate number and color." Mr. Jagnat Bakshi told Amar. "It's a Chrysler 200 and it's blue. KNB408-New York. Take a picture of the gun Amar and send it to Google Drive."

"According to this picture the gun has something written on it Mr. Bakshi." Said Amar. "It says 'man 64.13N, -21.93W. If my guess is right, that could mean coordinates of where the man is. What country is that Cnatla?"

"That is Reykjavik Iceland Amar." Said Cnatla after asking the system. "Let's keep the picture of the gun and decide when to go to Iceland Amar. In the meantime let's go and get Shanta," Said Cnatla.

They walked to Terminal 2 and waited in the arrivals area. Over the loudspeaker they said, "JetBlue flight 220 has just arrived from Tokyo." Then, "South African Airways flight 523 from Cape Town South Africa has just arrived."

Amar had a big sign he made with cardboard that said "Amar" so Shanta could identify him. A call came in to his cell phone from Shanta. "Amar, I'm in Customs, I'll be out in 5 minutes. See you soon. Bye."

"It's good Shanta's South African cell phone is working in America." Amar said to Cnatla.

"There she is. There's Shanta coming out now." Said Amar.

"You are correct Amar. The system gave me that image." Cnatla said.

Amar approached. "Shanta this is Amar. Welcome to America!" Shouted Amar with enthusiasm. They both embraced each other.

"I have a GSM phone and I was able to buy an AT&T SIM card in Cape Town. That's how I was able to call you when I arrived." Shanta expressed. "I also exchanged some of my South African rands for US Dollars there. I don't need to see currency exchange here."

"Very resourceful," explained Amar to Shanta. "Was your flight pleasant?"

"There was some turbulence as the plane was descending approaching Kennedy and that was a bit frightening otherwise everything went fine. The food was great. I had fried chicken with mashed potatoes and some green beans. I bought a bottle of Rosé wine for $2 and shared it with the person in the seat next to me. She told me she was coming to New York to see the Freedom Tower and that one of her brothers died on 9/11 2001 in 2 WTC or the south tower.

"We should all go see the Freedom Tower one day," said Mrs. Cathy Bakshi.

"That would be a very good idea for renewing the spirit," said Mr. Jagnat Bakshi.

"Since Anthony is at your house dad (Mr. Bakshi), Shanta and me will go back to your house. What do you think of that dad?" Said Amar.

"It's perfectly fine with me and your mother Amar. I consider you my son and I hope you feel that I can be your father-your secondary father." Mr. Bakshi told Amar. "Let's get your luggage in the trunk of that car Shanta," Mr. Bakshi said, pointing to a taxi.

Everybody got in the taxi and the driver headed for the Bronx. The weather was nice and sunny. Amar was looking around wondering- wondering about his cognition.

"It seems they are controlling mentally from the subconscious and making it look like they control physically with the word." Amar directed his words to Cnatla. "The entity 'intelligence' is to blame.'"

Cnatla said, "Who are they and why would they do that?" Testing her boss Amar.

"They have to be the devil, the Antichrist, and Lucifer Cnatla. Intelligence personified could be the problem also. I also blame time Cnatla which may have been established with the death of Jesus." Said Amar.

"How many more minutes to the home Amar?" Said Shanta

"The house is coming up on the right Shanta. Stop at that tree by the driveway driver. Okay we're here. How much driver?" Said Amar.

"That would be $55 sir."

"I will pay Amar." Said Mr. Jagnat Bakshi.

"I have a $100 bill driver. Do you have change?"

"Certainly, here is forty-five." Said the driver.

"Here take this five." Said Mr. Bakshi, returning $5 to the driver.

"Thank you sir excellency, have a wonderful day." Said a very happy driver.

Mrs. Bakshi used her keys to open the door and saw that Sarah was asleep on the sofa with the TV on. She used the walkie-talkie to talk to Anthony.

"Anthony we're back from the airport. Shanta is here." Said Mrs. Bakshi.

"Mom did you tell Shanta I gave Amar the switch for the man?"

"Shanta does not know about the switch that Amar has to use with the man." Said Mrs. Bakshi. "Shanta, Anthony gave a switch to Amar that he has to use with the man to activate his heart computer. We have to go to Reykjavik Iceland to see if the man is there."

"So we're not going to Canis Major now Amar?" Said Shanta.

"It's best we go to Reykjavik," said Cnatla. "The man may have a problem."

"I want to see my parents in Queens Amar," said Shanta.

"Tomorrow we'll go see them Shanta. In the meantime I will make a reservation for Reykjavik." Said Amar. "You stay in New York Shanta. Cnatla and me will go to Iceland to search for the man. What do you say about going in the living room and watching CNN."

Mr. Bakshi turned on the television to CNN. Amar knew Air Canada had a flight to Reykjavik and he called them on the home phone at the airport LaGuardia. There was a flight to Reykjavik with a connection in Montreal, Quebec and it was on Thursday so he made a reservation for two-him and Cnatla.

"Okay Cnatla. I made the reservation to Reykjavik. The flight is on Thursday at 8 a.m." Said Amar. "Everyone! I have to go to the pharmacy to get some medications."

Psychotropics were vital for Amar's mental illness and he knows he has to be medication compliant to keep his sanity. He took a taxi outside in front of the house to Wakefield Pharmacy. When he arrived he went to the counter.

"Can I have a refill of these medications please?" Said Amar.

"Okay you have Risperdal, Seroquel, and Luvox. How are you paying?" Said the pharmacist.

"I am paying with Rockland Medicaid and Affinity. Is that okay here in the Bronx?" Said Amar

"Let me enter the card number and sequence number in the terminal. Can I have the card please?" Said the pharmacist.

"Here it is," said Amar.

The pharmacist entered the card number and it seems everything went through successfully.

"You're fine Mr. Bakshi. Let me go in the back and prepare your medications. I'll be finished in 5 minutes." Said a confident pharmacist.

The pharmacist returned in 10 minutes. "Here you are. Everything is paid for Mr. Bakshi." The pharmacist said to Amar.

It was a cool 75 degrees and Amar had his sneakers on so he decided to jog home. It took about 12 minutes to jog the half a mile distance with several breaks of walking. He approached the home, slowed down, stopped, and rang the doorbell.

"Hi son. Did you get your medications?" Mrs. Bakshi said as she opened the door for Amar.

"Yes mom. I used my Rockland County Medicaid and there wasn't a problem authenticating it despite the location." Amar said with a look of accomplishment and admiration.

"What is that in the skies above Cnatla? It looks like a pyramid. Is that computer P1 Cnatla?" Uttered Amar.

"Correction Ron, that is Pyramid P1. 1/4 of the pyramid is the computer, remember?"

"Yes I remember now Cnatla, and 3/4 of the pyramid is to separate different life-forms according to type." Said Amar. "According to my paranoia Cnatla, the physical movement is an excuse to suppress sexual response."

"That is a logical conclusion." Said Cnatla. "And that policy is causing our physical infirmities. We can all blame the educated people for this Amar."

"I think they hold on to a forgotten reservation as a job to control the unknowing Cnatla." Expressed Amar. "Shanta I'm going to bed because tomorrow we got to go to our parents in Queens,"

"Okay I'll see you tomorrow Amar. Good night." Shanta, yawning as she spoke.

"I'm going up to sleep Cnatla, what are you going to do?" Said Amar.

"I'm going to transfer myself to computer P1 Ron. Good night." Cnatla yelled upstairs to Amar. "Good night Shanta and Mr. and Mrs. Bakshi...Computer P1, transport me to pyramid P1." Cnatla vanished and returned to Pyramid P1. Sarah said goodnight to Anthony with the walkie talkie and she and her FBI friends went home.

"I think they all left honey. You can close the front door." Said Mr. Bakshi to Mrs. Bakshi.

"Good night Shanta and Amar." Said Mrs. Bakshi. "Good night Jagnat," said Mrs. Bakshi. They cuddled up with each other. "Our son Anthony will be okay right hubby?"

"He must really feel betrayed under the house in isolation for so long Cathy." Said Mr. Bakshi. "He said the anxiety attacks forced him to go down there right Cathy?"

"That's what he said Jagnat." Replied Cathy. "I'm going to put the clock radio to sleep on some classical music. I'm setting the alarm for 6:30 a.m. There. Give me a goodnight kiss."

They kissed each other and in twenty minutes the silence of the night put them to sleep. They can sleep well knowing that their son Anthony is safe. The night was cool with a cool breeze and you could hear an owl hooting outside. The aliens formed some type of formation of lights with their spaceships in the sky. On occasion you could hear a low frequency sound of about 30 Hertz. If you're outside once in a while a mosquito may bite. A car passed by with someone playing reggae with an amplified subwoofer. There must be a correlation with the 30 Hertz. Maybe they were trying to lower the heart rate so we could sleep. It's important to nurture yourself and others even though you're no longer a baby. Soon everyone was asleep. Below the house Anthony was asleep also. The Martians take good care of him.

Chapter 6

When the morning arrived a bird was chirping and everybody woke up around 7:00 AM. Mrs. Cathy Bakshi went to the kitchen and started preparing breakfast. Soon Shanta was down there also and was helping her. They decided to make sausage and eggs with toast. Society is so inhumane to create food from animals thought Shanta and looked like she wanted to cry. Mrs. Bakshi read her mind intuitively. "It's okay honey, life is an illusion and Krishna wouldn't harm any creature." Said Mrs. Bakshi. You could see Shanta develop a smile. Mr. Bakshi and Amar came down just when they were finished making breakfast.

"How is my lovely Saraswati doing this morning?" Mr. Bakshi said to his wife Cathy. Saraswati is a goddess worshipped throughout India.

"Saraswati knows you love her Jagnat and I'm jealous," said Cathy with coy. "I know you love me Jagnat, otherwise we would have separated a long time ago. Although we had misunderstandings Jagnat, Krishna kept us together with reason. Also now that you know where our son Anthony is, we can also rejoice. Isn't it ironic how you reference a goddess and I reference a god?"

"It's like we have to be with each other no matter what Cathy," said Jagnat. "I have more of a reason to live because of Anthony."

"The sausage and eggs are good Amar. How do you like it?" Said Jagnat.

"They're very nice father. I'm glad the sausages are not beef." Said Amar. "How do you like the breakfast Shanta?"

"Very good Amar. I'm glad Auntie Cathy made the effort." Said Shanta. "Next time I will make dahl and roti for everyone. Call Mom and Dad in Queens at Indra's house Amar. Tell them we're coming."

"Okay. That's 1-718-555-2305," recited Amar as he punched the number in his cell phone. The phone rang several times then Indra answered…

"Hello Indra speaking, who is this?"

"This is your nephew Amar Auntie Indra. Me and my sister Shanta will be coming today to see our parents staying at your house. How are they doing there?"

"All this time you haven't come to see me Amar. What happened? Your parents are doing great here in Queens and they are anxious to see you. How are your parents there in the Bronx Amar?"

"They are okay with the understanding that my parents are not really them. They are elated that they found Anthony under the house and hope that he can come up to the surface. These moments can be very heartbreaking and lovely at the same time."

"Your father and mother told me about Anthony. We believe he is Krishna." Said Indra.

Aliens that have approached the Earth believe that Anthony is Krishna according to what Shanta knows from the signals she received from them. For some reason the aliens believed I was Krishna but that is not right." Said Amar.

"Maybe the shadow of Anthony's conscience was with you when you were in the house and that created a link to the aliens because Anthony needed a body to enable his transmission to them." Said Indra.

"I called the taxi Amar. The base said they'll be here in 5 minutes." Said Shanta.

"Okay we'll be there soon Auntie Indra," said Amar and they hung up the phones.

There was a car horn blowing outside and Shanta moved the blind from the window and could see the taxi. "Our taxi is here brother. Let's go." Said Shanta.

"Open the door for them." Said Mrs. Bakshi to Jagnat.

"Okay honey. You two have a safe trip and call me when you reach." Said mister Jagnat.

"Bye." Said Amar.

"Bye Bye." Said Shanta.

They walked up to the taxi and opened the back door of the Subaru Impreza. "112-05 Quantum Avenue, Queens driver," Amar said after they both sat down in the back seat. "How much would it be driver?"

"What village of Queens is that?" Said the driver.

"Forest Hills." Said Amar.

"That would be $15 and $5 for the Whitestone bridge." Said the driver. "The economic system is really a burden to life isn't it?"

"I think everyone can agree with that but what conspiracy keeps it going?" Said Shanta. "It definitely is controlling our movements in the environment and when we encounter each other?"

"I think it's a mental gang control instead of a direct connection of a joint just like the engine and the link to the transmission of the cars." Said the driver.

Amar said, "That makes a lot of sense driver because it's an indirect control and you really cannot verify the truth due to lack of contact. Isn't this the Whitestone Bridge we're on now?"

"Yes that's correct we're entering Queens." Said the driver. "We're on the Whitestone expressway right now."

"The spaceship to the east of us is approaching and is firing weapons on the ground." Said Shanta. "It looks like they're firing weapons at a military Convoy."

"Some airforce jets to the west is approaching," Said Amar. "Just keep on track to the destination driver."

One of the Jets fired a missile at the spaceships and a shield emerged from one of the ships without a detonation at impact. The ship fired back with what appeared to be a particle beam weapon and destroyed two of the planes. Military logistics at the ground radioed to the remaining plane, "Come back to base immediately, cease weapons firing. Do not attempt to engage spacecraft again."

"I can handle this control. Let me do this." Said the pilot. "I want to try to test my new Ultra Destroyer 1 beam guidance missile."

"This is a direct command soldier. Return to base!"

"Sorry I did not hear that." The pilot pretended. "You want me to fire the Ultra Destroyer 1? Control I cannot hear you." He pretended.

"I have a lock on the spacecraft control. Ultra Destroyer 1 launched."

In less than one second there was an impact on the spacecraft. The ship appeared to be wobbling out of control but stabilized. The spacecraft returned fire with the particle beam weapon and the Air Force jet was destroyed.

"We lost three good pilots and fifty million dollars worth of military equipment," said ground control command to his crew. "It seems we have to find a non-violent solution."

Amar, Shanta and the driver had to steer away from debris falling from the sky. "It looks like our friends the Aliens can safeguard themselves Shanta." Amar said looking deeply in the eyes of his sister.

Chapter 7

Melissa at Green Hills was wondering how Amar was feeling so she called Amar on his cell phone.

Ring...ring...ring...

"Hello this is Amar."

"Hello Amar, this is Melissa. How are you doing?"

"I'm doing fine Melissa. How is Ruthie?"

"Ruthie is fine. Why aren't you asking about me?"

"I'm the one with the mental illness Melissa. I'm sure you're fine."

"You're right I'm fine Anthony. Things are okay at Green Hills. Are things safe there in the Bronx? Do you have enough of your medications?"

"I had to renew my supply and that went okay at the pharmacy." Said Amar. "Me and my sister Shanta are in Queens right now. We're here to visit our parents that came from India. Cnatla and I are planning to go to Reykjavik tomorrow. I have a special mission to accomplish."

"Who is Cnatla?" Said Melissa.

"She is the Emissary of my system."

"Okay Anthony. Whatever. If you have any problems don't hesitate to contact me. Bye."

"Bye Melissa. Bye."

"Sir we're approaching the house," the driver said to Amar.

"That's it at the corner driver," Amar said. "You can stop here. Here's $20 and $5 for yourself. Thank you very much."

"Y'all have a wonderful visit and, see you young lady," the driver told Shanta.

Shanta got out the car quickly and ran to the door in excitedness and rang the doorbell. Her aunt Indra came to the door. "Oh I'm so excited to see you Shanta. How are you? Where is your brother Amar?"

"I'm right here Auntie Indra. You're looking so well. I'm very glad to see you. We brought our luggage for our trip to Reykjavik tomorrow. Mom and Dad inside mausii?"

"Yes Bhaanjaa." Said Indra. "Balram...Pamela! Shanta and Amar are here. Come in both of you please."

Shanta and Amar entered the living room and were greeted by Balram and Pamela. "How are you my children. You finally made it here," their father Balram said to them. "Your mother and I have been anxious to see you two. I guess you were busy with Anthony in the Bronx."

"Anthony's spirits are up and my parents there are happy that they found him," Amar said.

"We communicate with him with a walkie-talkie," said Shanta. "We're going to see if we can find the man in Reykjavik tomorrow. We believe he's being held captive."

"There are rooms available for you and Shanta Amar. Come now I'll take both of you upstairs," said Indra.

Amar and Shanta followed Indra upstairs. "This is your room Shanta and over here is your room Amar," said Indra. "Turn on the fans if you need to. The bathroom is down the hall to the right."

"Auntie Indra I need an iron to iron my pants and shirt for tomorrow." Said Amar.

"I'll bring it from my bedroom. Just hold on a minute."

Indra went to her bedroom and got the iron and gave it to Amar.

"Give me the iron after you're done brother. I need to iron my dress." Said Shanta

"I'll be done in 10 minutes Shanta." Said Amar.

Amar started ironing and suddenly his cell phone began to ring. "Hello, this is Ravi at the India consulate; how are you doing Amar?"

"I'm not fine Ravi. I'm worried about the man. Tomorrow I'm going to Reykjavik to try to find him. You have any ideas about him or where he might be?"

"Why did you choose Reykjavik Amar?" Said Ravi.

"Someone held us up with a gun and there was a clue on it. There were coordinates on it pointing to Reykjavik. Since the man is associated with a gun we assumed it meant him." Amar told Ravi.

"You're all pretty lucky. I'm glad none of you got shot. I assume it was the driver. How did you all disable him?" Asked Ravi.

"My mother Cathy had a can of pepper spray. We didn't call the police because we felt they and the FBI were involved. They're trying to get the switch that Anthony gave us for the man." Said Amar.

"What kind of switch and what would it do Amar?" Said Ravi.

"It's a lighted automotive switch with a transistor that has to be powered with 12 volts. It is supposed to activate his heart computer." Said Amar.

"This may be a dangerous trip Amar. I want you to go with a member from RAW. I'm sending him over now. Okay?" Said Ravi.

"I agree Ravi. It might be too much for me to handle. Send your agent. It's okay. Sarah from the FBI might have something to say about that, however."

"I'm going to call Sarah now Ravi."

Amar dialed the number on his phone and Sarah's phone began to ring. Sarah reached for the phone in her purse. "Hello. This is Sarah. Whom may I have the pleasure of speaking with?"

"Good morning Sarah. This is Amar. How are you? I'm the one who's lucky to have the pleasure of speaking with you."

"What's up?" Said Sarah.

"I'm doing fine honey. I'm going to Reykjavik tomorrow with Shanta and Ravi from the India consulate said I should walk with a member of RAW. That person will meet me today here. I'd like to know what you think of that. Mainly if you'll be able to cooperate with the agent?"

"That shouldn't be a problem assuming he's reasonable. As you know I don't like to keep secrets and I'm hoping he doesn't keep important information from me."

"I don't see why India and America cannot cooperate. We surely do not want to create any diplomatic problems." Said Amar.

"Look. Our main objective is to secure the man safety. Isn't that agreed upon?" Said Sarah.

"I agree Sarah. That's a mutual understanding." Said Amar. "I'm going to give a call to Kismet now and see what she says Sarah. Bye Bye."

Amar didn't know Kismet's number so he checked on Facebook to use messenger. There had to be a difference of time between Kismet's information and Amar"s information to retrieve the lie of feelings in the mind that the truth of reality erases. The stress of the time difference of the lie initiated the call with the power of thought applied to Amar's hands. Within a few moments Kismet answered her cell phone. "Hello Amar. This is Kismet. How are you doing?"

"I'm doing okay Kismet. Can you change to video chat?"

"Okay how is that Amar. Can you see and hear me well?"

"I'm going to Reykjavik tomorrow with Shanta and the India consulate says they would like a member of RAW to accompany us. What's your opinion?"

"The doorbell is ringing let me check it. It might be him. Hold on for a moment Kismet." Said Amar.

Surely enough, it was the member of RAW. "Hi this is Prem from RAW. The India consulate sent me and you seem to be, according to your looks Amar. Am I right?"

"Please come in Prem. I have a friend from RAW on the phone in India. Her name is Kismet. Do you know her?" Said Amar.

Amar turned on the speakerphone.

"Let me talk to her for a moment. I believe I do know her. Kismet. Are you 305782?"

"It's amazing how you remembered my agency number Prem. How are you?"

"I'm fine Kismet. I'll be going to Reykjavik tomorrow. That seems exciting. How are the aliens in India?"

"Everywhere I turn they want to know about Anthony. How is he doing Amar?"

"Anthony's fine. I'm hoping to meet the man in Reykjavik. Maybe he can stop Anthony's anxiety attacks so he can come to the surface. His parents in the Bronx are glad to know where he is and that he's well. Also since you know Prem, I guess I can trust him Kismet."

"Okay I don't want to keep you too long on the phone Amar but Prem update me on what you discover, especially what you know about US intelligence. Have a safe trip to Reykjavik tomorrow Amar. Bye." Kismet hung up the phone.

"Indra, do you have any beer in the fridge?" Said Amar. Indra looked in the fridge and saw a bottle of wine. There was a six pack of Corona next to the fridge.

"Do you want beer with ice or chilled wine Amar?"

"I'll go for the beer with ice. Please don't trouble yourself. I am coming to get it Indra."

Amar walked slowly from the living room to the kitchen while observing the passing walls feeling for his identity since his personality is rarely invoked. He came to the conclusion that the Jews were the unrecognized passing or clear-probably water and time combined. Are they causing the breach of integrity?

Amar always got the impression that people are all nice to him but little does he know there are many vile people among them that never want to admit that. "Does anyone ever breach your integrity Prem?"

"They asked me for a need that they should provide for themselves like money and self-understanding and they want me to agree with their arrogance. These people say they're no longer your friends so quickly without thought Amar."

"I think they lack self-respect because they destroyed their own character intentionally in the process of deceiving others," Said Shanta. "As an example, if their life is in danger they wouldn't think of protecting your life first because they believe they are more important than anyone else."

"Here's a glass of wine Shanta," said Indra. "The wine is from Italy but it was bottled in California."

"I really like the taste of the wine," said Pamela. "But wouldn't you prefer a wine made and bottled in India?"

"That would be good for the Indian economy since there would be more jobs." Said Balram. "You have the switch for the man for tomorrow right Amar?"

"I do Dad. I also have a variable power supply for the switch. And also I bought a laptop computer for the man in case we find him. They're trying to confuse the technology so the man would not understand and maybe this laptop will give the man some power over his mind and truth."

"Cnatla this is Amar, can you hear me?" He said on his watch.

"Yes Amar, I hear you-this is Cnatla."

"I'm confused. Am I taking you or Shanta to Reykjavik?"

"We're all confused as to what happened to the data correlation of the information. It seems you were taking me but then you thought you were taking Shanta. Amar take Shanta. I can transport myself anywhere if you need me including Reykjavik."

"Roger that Emissary. I'm going to take my sister Shanta. Some type of psychological distortion seemed to have taken over before and misdirected my mental processes."

"Since the physical is transparent to your mind Amar, some of it may have materialized in it and caused damage to your brain. I'm running a scan right now of your brain..."

"According to the system scan, a small part of your cerebellum is damaged as if something foreign tried to materialize. Did you have any numbness in the left side of your body Amar?"

"Yes Cnatla. About a week ago there was some numbness in my fingers on the left arm. If it was a stroke I recovered well."

"For now everything seems good Amar and if there's further unusual sensations just let me know. We have to know the reason for this. In the meantime go to bed Ron. Tell Shanta too. You have to go to Reykjavik tomorrow."

Cnatla said, "Disengage comlink system." The system disconnected Cnatla's communication with Amar.

Sara called Indra's house phone. "This is Indra. Who is this?"

"This is Sarah Indra. How are you. Goodnight. What is Amar doing?"

"Amar and Shanta are in bed. They have to sleep because they're going to Reykjavik tomorrow Sara."

"Indra, tomorrow please tell Amar I emailed him a file containing pictures of what the man may look like. According to my sources there is a strong possibility that he may be in Reykjavik."

"Okay Sarah I'll do that for you. It's late and you have a good night and sleep well."

"Goodnight Indra...Bye."

Back at the home of the Bakshi's, Anthony wished his father and mother good night via the walkie talkies. "We'll solve the problem for the man Dad and Mom. I'm very confident in Amar."

"Goodnight my dear son. We will get you out of there from under the house." Cathy said. "What are the Martians up to?"

"The main thing that they provide for me is psychotherapy to provide reasoning and logic to prevent compulsions. They also interface my mind with their computers so that they will have a better understanding of life and how it relates to the unknown that effect reality. This is done virtually so there are no restraints with wires and I can move around freely. They know the Aliens are looking for Krishna and I may very well be him and they are considering what may be best for me. They think the mother Earth may be my consort that was killed by God and that the moon may be my daughter. The present insanity faced by the human race is directly related to the moon. You all have a good night. I know it's late now."

"Good night son," said Jagnat his father. "We'll talk to you tomorrow."

Cathy and Jagnat went upstairs and went to bed after brushing their teeth and urinating.

"Put the clock radio on the classical station Jagnat and set it to sleep for one hour. Set the alarm to 7 a.m," said Cathy.

"Just one moment honey. Okay all done," said Jagnat to his wife. "Let me cover you with the blanket. There, that's good, we're both under."

"You want the air conditioner on Jagnat?"

"No Cathy, it's cool enough in here," said Jagnat.

Both of them remained quiet for about 10 minutes and somehow fell asleep at the same time. There was a brief shower and the temperature dropped about 10 degrees. You could hear a bird singing as it took refuge near the gutter. A squirrel in the attic was rustling back and forth as if it was confused by the sound of the rain and the chill. There was a sense that the soul of the earth felt secure in the darkness. After about 1 hour the clouds moved away from the sky and the stars were shining. Alien ships were flying back and forth with unpredictable patterns. I think they were trying to create sensible association of the unassociated physical forms so the spirit can make sense to function. Believing by seeing unassociated physical forms next to each other may be causing damage to the mind and that is why Anthony may be having anxiety attacks. Anthony did say he learned a lot from the anxiety attacks. One thing being thinking of the lie creates the truth which removes the feelings of the lie and forming something material. To turn something that is truth back into the lie you would actually have to feel the material or truth with your body. The anxiety attacks may be related to the gnats in the house that are so fast you can't hit them with your hand. They may be attacking the mind in some way.

The alarm clock turned on at 5 a.m. and Amar got up and woke up Shanta. "Shanta it's time to get up. We got to go to the airport. Our flight is at 8 a.m."

Indra woke up early. "Amar! I made breakfast for you and Shanta. Please come down," Indra yelled. "Also Prem, please come down for breakfast also!"

"I hear you Indra. I'm coming down immediately," said Prem. "This is great Indra. Fried eggs, sausage and toast?" Prem said with disbelief.

"What makes you think you're not worth it Prem?" Indra said sarcastically. "Please sit down and enjoy this meal. Make me happy for my effort."

Shanta and Amar came down the steps together and said good morning to Indra and Prem. "Breakfast smells good auntie Indra," said Shanta. "Amar sit down with Prem and let's enjoy breakfast. Sara emailed you pictures Amar"

"Guess who is here," said Pamela as Balram followed. "We don't want to disappoint anyone by sleeping too much. Did everyone have a good night sleep?"

"Everyone slept well Pamela," said Indra. "I always wondered what happened in our sleep Balram. Any thoughts on that Dr. Balram?"

"I think we time travel in our sleep going back in the past before our birth to find out who we were," said Dr. Desai.

"Why would we want to know who we were Balram?" Said Indra.

"I think we're curious about what's next. We want to know our destiny so that we can control it to avoid difficult encounters. We want to set the time and place and form of our next birth. Prem, it's time to take Shanta and Amar to the airport. You have the money to pay for your reservation Amar?" Said Dr. Desai.

"Yes Father. I have the money to pay for Shanta also. System can you page Cnatla for me?"

"Cnatla is still asleep Ron. I'll have her contact you later. Shanta did you pack your laptop in your carry-on?" Said DacDad.

"Yes system, I also have the 220v adapter plug for Iceland. I believe the laptop adapter is designed for 220 volts also. It's strange how the status quo does not provide us information that we could be certain of. What do you think of the status quo system?"

"I know that the status quo would like me to be under its control. If I want to I could destroy them but I'm not sure who they are so I also want to learn from them Shanta. I'm not sure that if I harm them I would be harming myself in the process. Like you said they don't provide us information we can be certain of. The media is a major player in this deception that the status quo controls. Part of this control is the Illuminati and the Freemasons but we have to make them admit this. We have to have some degree of confidence that we are thinking and perceiving the correct way to detect the information that we need. Amar is a paranoid schizophrenic and nobody admits the validity of the paranoia because that will unveil that there is a conspiracy. I think the spirit feels it's immune from touching itself but it doesn't realize that this is wrong. I don't know for sure who they are but in this way they can touch it whenever they want. Because of this people are afraid to look at each other especially when they're in the train or the bus. They made the spirit afraid to look at itself or touch itself and that is why people are going around wondering where to go or what decision to make with respect to time. They don't want the sexual nature of a woman to be with Amar because that will empower his mind to think more clearly. Did Amar ever tell you how women avoided him in public, like the pretty looking ones Shanta?" Said the System.

"We can't blame them System. I'm sure you know that. We have to understand why the paranoia, as we are hinting at right now, is not verified." Said Shanta.

"I understand that Shanta. The paranoia is not verifiable because of physical change of feelings that cannot be seen because time is not linear. Time does not go through the flesh because of pain but the paranoia goes through the flesh without pain and it sends time through the flesh and time doesn't like that. Because of this Shanta, God and time sees Ron along with all mentally ill people as a great enemy since paranoia can control the rate and direction of time," said the System.

"I'm ready," said Prem. "Let's go in the car Shanta and Amar. I called Kismet. She said the R&AW should be updated on everything. Both of you have your cell phones, correct?"

"Correct. Let's go Shanta," said Amar. "Bye mom and dad."

"Bye son. Take care of yourself," said Pamela. "They're leaving now Indra!"

"God bless both of you." Said Indra. "Now go on now. May Krishna be with the three of you."

"Startup that Monte Carlo!" Said Amar to Prem. "Isn't this the coolest car you've ever seen Shanta?"

"Cars are ridiculously too expensive today Amar. I have a love for the Cherokee, the Jeep Cherokee."

"Okay everybody has their seatbelts on?" Said Prem.

"Of course chauffeur-we're good," said Shanta after observing Amar.

"We're going to Terminal B of LaGuardia Airport for Air Canada," said Prem. After ten minutes he said, "We're entering the Grand Central Parkway. We should take about 20 minutes to reach East Elmhurst, New York."

"Yeah," said Shanta. "What's your reaction Amar?"

"Perfectamente Excellency. I walked with my Radio Shack Optimus digital camera. Did you walk with yours Shanta?"

"Mine is a Vivitar and it has optical zoom and can take 10 megapixel pictures. Did you remember your USB cable Amar?"

"I did walk with my USB cable. You don't have yours?"

"I don't think I have mine Amar. Is yours a micro B to type A?"

"Yes Shanta. If you need to charge your phone or connect to the computer just let me know. Also you may be able to buy one at the airport."

Amar's cell phone began to ring and vibrate and he reached for it on his waist and answered it. "Hello. Amar speaking, who is this?"

"Amar this is Ruthie at Green Hills. What are you up to?"

"I'm sorry I did not inform you Ruthie. I'm taking a trip to Iceland. I'm okay, I've been taking my medication."

"Why are you going to Iceland?"

"I think the man is there and I have to free him from captivity. I know that sounds paranoid but we have strong reason to believe that he is there. My mental state is fine and I'm not psychotic. What's the alien activity like in Haverstraw?"

"There's flashes in the sky at night and there are sounds like there are bombings in the distance. My compass is showing that north is east." Said Ruthie.

"The Earth's magnetic field shifted. It may be due to an unknown power source emulating in the planet. Alien transmissions I've received indicates that there is an effort to resolve something that relates to god and mental illness." Said Amar to Ruthie.

"What's special about you Amar is that you are able to monitor your mental state as if you have a secondary mind. Pay close attention to your primary mind and make sure you don't decompensate and do anything irrational."

"Got it Ruthie and thanks. What would you like me to bring for you from Iceland Ruthie?"

"I heard there's a lot of volcanoes there. Can you bring me a volcanic rock?"

"If it's not too big or heavy it should be okay. What would you want with a volcanic rock?"

"I don't know really Amar. For sentimental reasons I guess. I had a dream actually that I was cold and lost and volcanic rocks kept me warm. I plan to use it in the fireplace."

"Very thoughtful Ruthie. Call me on the phone to remind me, okay?"

"What are you going to do when you have anxiety attacks Amar?"

"I'm walking with my sister Shanta. I'll talk to her whenever possible. I understand they speak English but their main language is Icelandic. In case of any problem I should be able to communicate with any psychiatrist or the police or paramedics. I'm concerned that they don't care about my psychological security as if they don't want me to change the intelligence so it's hard to trust." Said Amar.

"Just for those reasons, be careful what paranoid things you say Amar because they could say you're insane and have to go in the hospital and I'm sure you do not want that. Many of them are just looking for a fault to act on because they don't want the mentally ill to have free expression and thought because the mentally ill can explain the conspiracy." Said Ruthie.

"I feel that the physical activity of the normal people are being controlled by my paranoid symptoms. They are avoiding worrying and this is why I cannot identify with them. If they would define the symptoms of paranoia with the worrying this would verify paranoia is controlling their behavior." Amar said. "Another thing is that time took the trust of Jesus with the cross and God acquired it. The death of Jesus was a disadvantage and not an advantage for us. It was a punishment for his freedom to live at his own pace and this is why they pushed and beat him when he was carrying the cross."

Amar's phone disconnected somehow.

"Okay this is terminal B of Air Canada," Prem said. "I'm stopping you at the curb. I'm going to park and come back."

"Okay Shanta let's go," Prem said. I'll get a trolley for the luggage. Here we go. Put it right there. I've got both of our ticket reservation so I'll tell them."

Prem returned in about 15 minutes.

"I got my ticket here. It is the same flight as both of you," said Prem. "You two seem to have forgotten that I was coming. I heard when Amar was making reservations over the phone, so I made one for myself on the same flight."

All three of them went to the ticket clerk.

"Hi. I'm Amar and she is Shanta Desai. I have two reservations for Reykjavik. This is Prem. He has his own ticket. I would like him to sit with us."

"Okay let me look for that in the computer Amar," said the ticket clerk. "Okay. Seats 20 D, E and F. Please put your baggage on the scale...It looks like nothing is overweight for you or Shanta Amar. You are also okay Prem. Go to the x-ray for body scanning over there please."

"Let's go over there to security Shanta and Prem." said Amar.

"Please empty your pockets and carry on and walk through this machine," said the officer.

Shanta and Prem went through the machine.

"You're cleared Shanta." Said the officer. "You're also cleared Prem."

Amar went through the machine.

"You're cleared Amar but what is this switch?"

"It's just a power switch a friend requested in Iceland for his computer," lied Amar.

"Okay once no terrorism is involved it is fine," said the officer.

Because the switch is for the man, Amar couldn't trust anyone because anyone could be conspiring against the man.

They headed for the gate to board the plane and they showed their boarding passes to the female attendant and entered the plane.

"Here's 20 D, E and F Amar," said Shanta and all three of them sat down after putting the luggages in the overhead compartments.

"Welcome aboard Air Canada. We will be arriving in Reykjavik in approximately 7 hours with a stopover in Quebec, Canada," the pilot said over the sound system. "Please put on your seat belts for takeoff."

"Looks like we're ready to go Shanta." Said Amar. "I'm having an anxiety attack."

"I know it's scary Amar," said Shanta. "Sit down and breathe and count three inhale and three exhale breaths. Don't worry I'm here with you Amar. I'm your sister, you can trust me. We're going to have a wonderful time in Reykjavik. Play some music through your walkman using the headphones."

"It's hard to listen to you and obey Shanta, but I'm going to listen to you and cooperate," said Amar with fear. "I'm thinking that they want to steal the switch from me."

"Who're they," asked Shanta.

"Those who I've already always suspected, the lovers of the soul using God or the Antichrist. They; time, intelligence and truth, want to disable the man because he would stop the love." Amar told Shanta fearfully.

"I know you're feeling fear Amar, I can see it in your eyes. Just try to relax and breathe regularly so that the fear will go away. Nobody is going to hurt you."

"The anxiolytics never worked that's why I don't take it. One benefit of the attack is that it helps me to reason about what's happening that is unknown. I think intelligence and the Antichrist is feeling fear when I have the attack," said Amar. "You have Melissa's number at Green Hills Shanta?"

"Yes I do Amar. Do you want me to call her?"

"Text her and tell her I'm having an anxiety attack but I'm under control."

The flight attendant stopped by: "You look worried. Can I be of any help sir?"

Amar answered in fear, "I just need a cup of water thank you. I'm having an anxiety attack."

"Okay I'll be back in a moment. You just relax," said the flight attendant.

In less than 2 minutes the flight attendant came back and gave him a cup of water with ice. "There you are sir. I hope you feel better. We will be taking off in 5 minutes."

"Please put your seats in the upright position and note the fasten seatbelt sign above your head," the pilot said over the speaker.

Melissa texted back to Shanta's phone. "There's a notification sound on my phone. It must be Melissa. Let me check it," said Shanta.

Melissa texted, "You'll be fine Amar, just relax. You've been through this many times, remember?"

"Text her 'I feel better Shanta. What's happening at Green Hills?'"

In about 20 seconds Melissa texted back, "Things are okay at Green Hills; just feel better okay?" Shanta read to Amar.

The plane started taxying. It went around the turn and stopped. After it stopped its engines powered up and the plane accelerated, taking off after nine or ten seconds.

"Those turbines have a massive amount of power Amar," said Shanta. "Did McDonald Douglas build these planes or a company in Canada?"

"I think they were made by Fleet Canada in Fort Erie, Ontario. I came across that here on a bulletin somewhere in the airport," said Amar. "By the way Shanta, my anxiety attacks have gone away mostly and I feel so relieved. I think my memory of others are changing their positions relative to me. This could mean I am turning my environment as I turn. Also my period of time used is not being recognized by others. The memory of my feelings are being lost in the process and it's causing fear."

"When you say changing their position Amar, it could be that means that they're preparing space before they move so they wouldn't be blocked before they reach where they're going. I get the feeling that your soul is giving back your feelings to the previous thing you were looking at so the mind and the feelings are opposite. It could be they're physically existing in the space of your nerves. You want some jelly beans Amar?"

"I would love some Shanta. I love jelly beans. Why don't you charge your phone in the USB port. Here's the cable."

"Thank you. Can you get my laptop out of the carry-on on the overhead bin?" Shanta asked Amar.

Amar reached above for the carry-on and removed the laptop.

"It's a Toshiba. Good choice." Said Amar. "What cloud storage service do you use? I use Amazon Drive."

"I use Google Drive," said Shanta. "I use the Google Chrome browser also."

"I use Windows 10 and the Edge browser but sometimes it doesn't work properly so then I have to switch to Chrome," said Amar. "It's very hard for many countries to upgrade to the latest operating system and many cannot even afford computers."

"So what's your solution bright boy?" Said Shanta.

"Shanta I think we should have many more exchange students from many countries so we can share our intellectual assets and create a balance of the economic system worldwide with the jobs created with cultural equilibrium."

"Don't you know people eat words when they talk Ron? That's how they learn in school, by eating words of the mind. They see the lie but they can't feel the lie and that's why they can't tell you anything. The lie is the difference of feelings which is the sin. When you feel the lie it becomes sin. However when you believe the lie it becomes love. I think the reason they have so much control is by controlling your brain computer of the system."

"What are they controlling the brain computer to do Shanta?" Said Amar. "MC 10-2B on the moon was created with a copy of my brain.

"Maybe they want it to disconnect from itself and disregard you Amar since I know you're very important to the system and the aliens."

"What do you believe the aliens want with Anthony Shanta?"

"From the analysis of their communication I think they want to conquer the personality 'sight' that the devil controls for the misallocation of physical things. That can be identified as wayward moving of the eyes as if the eyes are searching for its vision.'"

"Are you saying that 'sight' controls the movement of the eyeballs Shanta?'"

"Hold on Amar, I'm on Twitter and there's a live broadcast by the aliens. Wait. Let me connect my splitter so we both can listen with headphones at the same time. Plug in your headphones here."

"I'm hearing." Said Amar.

Alien comm; We are rupturing the silence right now thanks to the presets of the rap musicians with the turntables. I want you all to use your old cassette decks and record whatever you want. Play it because this will cancel the love of God detected as tape hiss indicating wasted energy. Our primary objective is to stop the love and restore the sight of Kali, the Hindu Goddess. The Aliens are the lenses in our eyes and the evil uses the focusing process to disrupt them with stress so they can't understand each other. The intelligence is using a physical state to disable us physically and it's due to God. You may feel incapable because there is no memory space to apply your own intelligence because the space is blocked by something physical.

"I guess there's a lot going on that we can't see in reality," said Prem. "Do you even believe what we think we are is true. The Freemasons are hiding a lot from us and they're guilty of silence since so much destruction happen in the world without sharing their knowledge. What is your conclusion using your paranoia Amar?"

"Well Prem, I think they're deleting our thoughts and memories so we can't construct the foundation of the conspiracy and we cannot even conceive that a conspiracy is happening. As for me my thoughts are physical and that puts me in a different category, I have to constantly think of how to validate my paranoia before I say it to a mental health worker so they wouldn't think I'm crazy and have to be in the hospital in a psychiatric ward. I believe by transposing the paranoia by inverting the intelligence the paranoia will become understandable. This can be as easy as contradicting or inverting the intelligence of what is said to you and this can work with a schizophrenic or someone normal. For example if I say 'The cop is a criminal,' you can simply say I don't believe that, validating reality.'"

Chapter 8

Ring...Ring. Amar's cell phone was ringing. "Hello, this is Amar speaking."

"Amar this is Sarah. How are you doing? Still in your flight?"

"We should be arriving in Quebec soon Sarah. What's up?"

"Anthony says he's coming to the surface within the hour. The aliens are going to shield him from the anxiety attacks. The aliens plan to take him to Canis Major after he had a brief time with his parents so you don't have to go there Amar and you should concentrate on the man. Where are you at now?"

"The plane is descending to land in Montreal right now," said Amar. "There appears to be a MiG 29 flanking the Air Canada...A second one has come into view," said Amar.

The pilot came on the speaker saying, "Please don't be alarmed passengers, the Russian MIGS are just there to guide us because of poor visibility to land."

"I heard what the pilot said Amar-he's lying. The info from my FBI sources believes China wants to shoot the plane down."

"What's India intelligence saying Prem?" Said Amar

"According to communication from Kismet, R&AW said I'm a risk to Chinese National Security because to be honest, I'm carrying the decryption software for their military launch codes for their ICBMs." Said Prem.

"Why would you be carrying that software Prem?" Said Shanta.

"The Chinese are trigger happy. I want the man to disable their military network so they will not start a world war, especially with India." Said Prem. "The Kremlin gave me this software and that's why the MIGs are there." Said Prem.

"Where do you plan to run the program?" Said Shanta.

"With the man's authorization, his heart computer of course," said Prem.

One of the stewardesses came to Prem and told him the pilot would like to see him after the plane has landed in Montreal. As the plane descended everybody was buckled in with seat belts. After about four minutes the airport could be seen as the runway approached. The MIGs departed right and left away from the Air Canada. The tires touched the runway and smoked and screeched as the brakes were engaged, slowing it down safely. After three minutes the plane stopped and in a few moments the airstair deployed at the rear of the aircraft. The stewardess took Prem to the cockpit to speak to the pilot.

"Why did you take that risk with the software and the plane, we could have been shot down?" Said the pilot. "The Canadian authorities are very concerned."

"Sir R&AW are taking the necessary precautions so there is no risk to Canada and its security," Explained Prem.

"We will be in Montreal for two hours before we take off to Reykjavik, Iceland. Canadian police will be monitoring you at all times. You're free to go." Said the pilot.

"Let's go hang out in the airport," said Shanta to Amar.

The three of them started moving in the terminal and noticed a coffee stand. "Who's for coffee," said Amar.

Prem and Shanta raised their hand one after the other. Prem said, "It's self-serve; let's help ourselves."

After they made the coffee they paid the clerk. "$3.75 please," said the cashier. A young girl that appeared to be fifteen. Amar paid with Canadian dollars he got from an ATM.

A police officer approached the three of them with a serious look on his face. "I understand the three of you are going to Reykjavik. I want to assure you that you're well protected here in Montreal. Please feel free to explore the airport."

"I feel like having a drink. Let's go to that bar over there," said Amar. "Bartender El Dorado and ginger ale on the rocks please!"

"I'd like a glass of chardonnay on the rocks please bartender," said Shanta.

"Can you give me a cold bottle of Beck's and a glass with ice please bartender," ordered Prem.

"That would be $11 for the three of you," requested the Bartender.

Amar produced $11 with $1 tip. "Sir, how long have you been working at Mirabel airport," Asked Shanta.

"About 5 years now," said the bartender. "What brings you all to Montreal?"

"This is our stop over. We're going to Iceland." Said Shanta. "I'm surprised your drinks are relatively inexpensive. Personally, what's your favorite?"

"Actually Miller beer from America is my favorite drink. A lot of travelers from America order that here. It is very tasty along with being very economical. You can get a bottle here for $2.50 Canadian money."

"Can I smoke in the terminal or I have to go to a designated area?" Amar asked the bartender.

"That room to your left is a smoking room. You can go there and have your cigarette." Said the bartender.

"Shanta and Prem I'll be back in 10 minutes. Let me go to have my cigarette." Amar said.

"Remember we have to get our flight so don't take too long," said Shanta.

"Amar seems to be unconcerned about his safety. That's a good thing considering he's a schizophrenic," said Shanta to Prem. "I must praise him for being able to function in the real world without psychotic behavior along with good communication skills.

Nobody wants mentally ill people locked up in institutions. I think the best thing for them is to remain medication compliant."

"Medication compliant means that you have to sacrifice your soul from being spontaneously reactive to stimuli and that's a hard thing to accept but I'm glad he's doing it," Said Prem.

"My daughter is a schizophrenic," said the bartender. "When she's off her psychotropics she's very aggressive and can be violent with criticism. You cannot be impulsive with a mentally ill person and you really have to be careful about what you say because they're very sensitive. I'm hoping the aliens would offer a solution for such a terrible illness. Here is your friend coming back now from smoking. Are you more like yourself now?"

"I was surprised that so many Canadians smoke because there was so many people in the smoking room. I mean I'm sure many of them were from another country but somehow my instincts were telling me they were Canadians," said Amar. "Let's go back to the plane, it's almost time for departure. It's been good to know you bartender. Now you have a good day sir."

They walked briskly to the gate of the Air Canada and entered the plane, going to their seats. A flight attendant verified who they were with a smile. "Looks like you people had a life-changing experience here in Montreal," She said. "Slow down, don't stumble you have time."

"Nice to be on the plane again," said Prem to Shanta and Amar. "I have security again knowing that I wouldn't be lost in the world. It's amazing how an enclosed space can change your feelings."

The pilot announced that they would be taking off in 5 minutes. "Please put on your seatbelts everyone and prepare for takeoff," said the flight attendant over the speaker. In a moment the toe vehicle hauled the plane to the runway. The engines of the plane revved up and the plane started accelerating. There was some anxiousness as people held their breath hoping that takeoff would be successful. In about two minutes the plane settled at 20,000 feet with a velocity of 500 knots.

Meanwhile in the Bronx, the aliens transported Anthony to the surface. Two of the Martians, a male and a female were also transported with Anthony. If you looked carefully you would notice some type of transparency around Anthony. This is to shield the control of belief coming from God and the devil, mainly to prevent love and anxiety by using his soul. Anthony looks like he was about 5 feet and 10 inches tall and the Martians both look like they were 5 feet. A messenger from one of the alien ships transported down to the surface where they were.

"Are you okay Lord Krishna. How do you feel?" The alien from the ship said to Anthony.

"Surprisingly I feel fine. I just have a little fear of the unknown. I guess I owe the man my life, would you know where he is?" Anthony said.

"We are now sure that he is in Iceland-Amar was right. We believe the government of Iceland has been protecting him and we will try to figure out where to rendezvous with him," the alien from the spaceship said with reassurance. "Be comforted with your parents Anthony, they love you very much."

Anthony spent some time discussing what the experience underneath the house was like to his parents. "What news were you abreast to most of all son?" Said Mr. Bakshi.

"Dad I was concerned about the war in Yemen and why there was so little media coverage about it and I also watched news about the war in Syria. The military really want to kill the aliens who are in the conscience of the human beings. They will never tell us what's going on since they caused the death of Christ. We will have to remove their lid to start the momentum of revelation. The main covenant of God is to keep love at all costs even if that means killing the man. Putting that in hindsight, I'm glad to see you dad and mom. I'm really breathless not really believing that this is really happening." Said Anthony.

"What I'm really concerned about son is how they use the spirit for their selfish motives. Everybody's farting because of the love they're doing and they want to keep that secret. I can see your justification for the motivation to stop this." Said Jagnat.

"We will do everything to encourage you son," said Cathy Bakshi. "I want you to have some of this okra with shrimps and rice I just made. "Sit on the table. I'll serve you."

"Gladly mom," said Anthony. "Emm, this is very good mom. You have some water?"

"Better yet, I have some Pepsi. I'm going to put some ice in a glass with it. La la em la. Here you go son, fresh from a can. Love shouldn't be used to get this." Said Cathy.

"This is the best food I've ate in years. You really can cook good mom. Thank you." Anthony gave her a kiss. "Mother Lakshmi is really with you Mom. Although I've been missing so long you really care for me." Anthony told her he loved her and gave her a hug. "The Martians said that fear of physical contact and the inability to make that contact can cause anxiety. This is why I am making a secondary contact with you Mom."

Jagnat was making a careful observation of his son. "I didn't think I would have a son that is Lord Krishna son. It's hard to believe that God would make you suffer. But then again if he is the Antichrist that would be understandable. I can now extrapolate the people in India are worshiping an antichrist. In fact the entire world is worshiping an antichrist in their churches and at home. If you are Krishna then I must be Vasudeva. You know thinking in hindsight, the love may be occurring with disorder that's why it cannot be detected, as thoughtless and meaningless actions of the body. Complementary thoughts that are destructive are being done by the identity 'Ann' with our actions such as breathing. Jews are using energy loss to disguise themselves. God is using theory to disable the human race and the media is controlled with this theory. Dirt is applied to love to establish his theory. Since you're not using mathematics in our communication we are vulnerable to the wrath of God.

"We are ready to transport you to the ship Anthony," said the alien from the ship. "What belongings would you like to take Anthony?"

"I'd like to take the power supply I built, it may be needed. I also would like to take a picture of mom and dad. I guess I wouldn't be needing a cell phone. Could you get the picture of mom and dad in my room mom, please."

"What was your room son," said Cathy. How did you know there was a picture there?"

"We have our abilities mom and I hope you don't mind the invasion of privacy," said Anthony. "According to my intelligence about you mom, you're very open to personal things and I must say I am also. I guess we adopted the ways of Dad. It's no secret to anyone that Dad loves you very much."

"Anthony were you aware that Amar replaced you when you went underground?" Said Cathy.

"Yes I did mom. It was necessary that Amar believe that you and dad were his parents. if you and dad knew that Amar was not your son, there was no telling where you and dad would go and leave me all alone here. The Martians had a plan that now is the time for revelation and patience was the most important thing. Conditions are now falling into place very quickly and today's computers are fast enough and have adequate memory to process all these changes for the sake of Earth life."

"Cathy! Sharon from the Indian Consulate is on the phone," said Jagnat. "She wants to talk to you honey. She wants to inquire about Anthony. Here, take the phone." Cathy took the phone from Jagnat.

"Hi Sharon from the India consulate," said Cathy. "Who told you about Anthony?"

"Sarah from the FBI told me about Anthony. We have to be aware of our Gods. If I'm right, he is Lord Vishnu. They're very excited in India about him. Reuters may have heard from Kismet and broadcasted the information here in India. The Indians are wondering what the aliens will do next. I know they're connecting our minds telepathically, that's why we're aware of things that we never said to each other. Is it true you have a tattoo on your ankle? Just wondering.

"Yes Sharon, it is of a cat. So who told you about it?"

"The aliens must have made me know that notification." Said Sharon. "I think they want me to ask you why you chose that tattoo so they can learn what it is related to as they monitor the universe. Since I believe I'm correct, why do you have that particular tattoo Cathy my dear?"

"I stepped on a kitten in the dark and I never saw the kittens but I heard it meow in pain and I'm hoping that it is still living a good life. The tattoo of the kitten signify my apologies to it and its blessings that I will have a good life." Said Cathy.

"So if I can psychoanalyze, the kitten knew you were sorry because you had a good life. Anthony represents the kitten's messenger like Christ was to his followers. Does that make sense Cathy?" Sharon said.

"You brought up a thought Sharon. I felt grief in my subconscious ever since that night I stepped on the kitten not knowing its fate."

"And that statement correlates with Anthony being missing for so long. Don't you agree?" Said Sharon.

"Sharon you are so correct and I have to conclude that there must be a plan in existence for life all this time and the quest to uncover the problem and to solve it." Said Cathy.

"Anthony we are ready to transport you to the ship and during our journey you will have opportunities to communication with your parents here on Earth," said the Alien. "Put on this tracking device on your wrist so we can monitor you at all times so you are not lost. Your power supply is already on board the ship so you can experiment on your electronics if you so wish to along the way to Canis Major. Will you be taking your test equipment?"

"I will be taking my Micronta multimeter from Radio Shack and my Goldstar oscilloscope. Also some discreet semiconductors and other parts. I'm walking with my Acer laptop also. Is there something else you think I should walk with?" Said Anthony to the alien.

"Well Anthony, maybe you can walk with your favorite pillow and a stuffed animal for comfort. What did the Martians say?"

"Well the Martians are giving me psychotropics for my mental health and they have provided a large supply for me. How long will the journey take to go and come?" Said Anthony.

"Maybe a few days to a week. I cannot be sure because I don't know what we'll encounter with God or the unknown Anthony," said the Alien.

"Alien what is your name? You didn't tell me your name?"

"I am known as Sae and my gender is female. I sincerely hope you like strong women. There are other humans aboard the ship so you might be able to find people of Interest."

"Sae, I am quite pleased to see you. You're quite beautiful for an alien and because of this my emotions are vulnerable. I am assuming I am worth a woman as you so please pardon my aloofness. What is your impression of a person such as I?"

"Well I am honored to be with a person who may well be Krishna and who is responsible for creation and I do feel you are quite seductive but there is my reservations for further investigation. To be honest I am turned on when you dance and you should know that if others dance like you the problems will be resolved. Thinking about it logically, you should walk with some of your dance music on compact disc and a boom box that you like. I like the one by RCA that you have. Of course we have our capabilities to play the music but I just thought that you might want to have something sentimental along the way. It is important that you have things made of earth materials." Said Sae.

"Well Sae, if my guess is right, you want me to do a lot of dancing. You would have to teach me because all I can do is freestyle." Said Anthony.

"Since the problem is classified as a mess, freestyle, which is random, is the most effective way of neutralizing it Anthony," said Sae. "There is no need for a dance with logical steps but if you insist I could try it with you. So as not to make you worry about learning to dance, our computers can create the algorithm from your freestyle and it is the algorithm we need to disable the Antichrist. The algorithm is a pulsed binary file to turn the beliefs on and off in the cosmos. Think of it as turning your radio on and off when it feels good to do so. At the same time we are processing the schizophrenia to create a logical structure of thought to apply the correct physical forces to life so that the spirits will have the correct feelings without fear."

"What do you think of Ron's website, or I should say Amar's website Anthony?"

"I can understand and appreciate his paranoia but the real world refuses to acknowledge it. Maybe he's being too explicit forcing an impression. Maybe he should be implicit so people can use their own reasoning to judge about the content. He didn't speak of being violent so I know he's not critical or insane. From the notes of his psychiatrist, I gathered that the psychiatrist feels uncomfortable because she cannot confirm the insanity as being true because she will lose her license if she supports him. I guess it's up to the aliens to protect the psychiatrist by showing proof of the paranoia. It is hard for a doctor to live and not admit that there is a God and a devil for that matter who may be causing the illness. Amar's heart is good and I like him because he has a conscience. He will not hurt the innocent because he knows he is a victim himself of the status quo. I pity the police whom have to comply by the law although they disagree with the government. Sae, what is law like in your world?"

"Anthony the only law we have is to comply to what is moral so there is no confusion as to how to act or treat others. All we use is compassion and that comes naturally with sentient beings such as ourselves. We have no jails but we have psychiatric hospitals for those who have trouble reasoning properly. They are free to think as they like as long as they are not a danger to themselves or others just like in your world Earth. Are you ready for transport to the ship?"

"Yes Sae. Are you ready martians for transport?"

"We are ready Anthony."

Cnatla came out of the house and said, "Are you all forgetting me Sae? Don't you remember I'm going too?"

"This is Sae. The five of us are ready for transport. Please initiate transport."

"Initiating transport Sae," said someone from the ship.

Within five seconds they were aboard the alien ship. Sae looked at what earthlings would call the captain of the ship. "Vorlon our guests are here."

"Their belongings have been transported already. Show them to their quarters Sae," said Vorlon. "Welcome aboard Anthony, Emissary Cnatla, Martians. We hope to make your stay aboard this ship as pleasant as possible. Just to let you know, Amar's plane has landed in Iceland. The angels of God are trying to kill him so we are monitoring his environment continuously. They have kept us in an oblivious state of mind. This is an attempt to elude us from how they are controlling. I am hoping that Amar finds the man so we can control the quiescence with the switch.

Chapter 9

Meanwhile in Iceland Amar, Shanta and the agent from RAW booked a room at a hotel and ordered dinner since it was about 5 p.m. in Iceland. The agent from RAW went outside for a cigarette and observed his surroundings. It was overcast but there was no rain and the temperature was about 50 degrees Fahrenheit with a slight wind of 5 miles per hour. Several crows flew over above them sending a message that something may be wrong- according to Prem's interpretation. Were they heading for something or fleeing from something or was this Prem's paranoia. After his cigarette Prem saw a food truck and went up and ordered coffee and a hot dog. He was thinking that maybe he would not eat the hotel dinner after this, regretting the additional cost for him. He reached quickly for his cell phone and called Amar and told him to cancel his part of the order. After that he felt much better that they would save money.

"Okay Shanta, how do we find out where the man is?" Said Amar in their hotel room. "We know he's in Reykjavik but where? Turn on the television Shanta. Maybe we can have some kind of clue of where to look. Check who's knocking on the door!"

Shanta opened the door. "Hi Prem, you had your cigarette?" Said Shanta.

"Yes I had my cigarette and a hot dog and soda-sorry, I meant a coffee. I see you're about to finish dinner. How's the chicken?"

"The chicken is great!" Expressed Amar. "Try a piece. Here. It's delicious."

Prem reached for a piece of chicken and ate like it was the last thing you had to eat on Earth. "I should be filled Shanta and I don't know why I'm eating more. My phone's ringing. I can feel the vibration, let me answer it. "Hello this is Prem, can I help you?"

"Hi Prem, this is Kismet, how are you? I understand you're in Iceland according to my intelligence sources."

"Of course, I thought you remembered we were planning this. I thought I had the bad memory." Said Prem.

"I remembered Prem. I was just checking to see your identity by how you reacted over the phone. You know how we agents are. Sarah gave me a tip about the man's location so I thought I should convey it to you."

"Okay Kismet, what is it?

"There is a US Navy Air Base called Keflavik nearby and I'm thinking it may be our target. The Russians are doing reconnaissance on it with their high altitude planes. Secret transmission from their satellites have been detected and decrypted. Sarah is supposed to give me a call with that information. What I can tell you right now is she believes the man is being transported from location to location within the area. We know this because there is a tracking device we are receiving signals from that has a pattern of time changes that can be extrapolated as an urgent situation of some kind. I think they're using him as bait for the aliens so they can destroy the aliens or any evidence of what the aliens have in mind assuming it's good. I think it is safe to say you can tell Amar to inform the aliens that a trap is being set for them. We have to figure out the nature of that trap to find out where the man is."

"Okay Kismet, I will inform Amar of your conclusion. Bye."

Amar said, "I overheard you Prem, who were you talking to?"

"I was talking to Kismet Amar. She said that the man is being shuffled from place to place in the area because she believes the US government is setting a trap for the aliens. Kismet is expecting a call from Sarah from the FBI with further information. I hope they don't charge her with espionage."

"What's going on?" said Shanta. "Sounds critical. Update me Amar!"

Meanwhile Sarah was having pizza at a pizza shop in Harlem close to her home. "What would you like to order Sarah?"

"Can I have a slice with sausage and a Pepsi in the can Dave. I'm not cooking tonight because I want to treat myself. I was thinking of making a sandwich at home but I changed my mind because I need this outdoors experience. I like the Police song on the radio. What station is that?"

"It's wnew-fm at 102.7. I didn't know you liked rock Sarah," said Dave.

"I know you think I like pop music and classical right? Sometimes I listen to rock sometimes, especially classical rock. I have a record of U2 or should I say a CD. I like that song 'With Or Without You.'"

"My favorite band is Journey," said Dave. "Don't Stop Believin' is my favorite song from them. I'm trying to learn the guitar. Here's your pizza and Pepsi Sara."

"Thank you. That's a big slice. It looks nice and the Pepsi feels cold too." Sarah walked to a table and took a seat to eat her pizza. Sarah heard a beep from her phone and checked for a text. It was a text from the defense secretary at the Pentagon which read: Sarah, R&AW contacted me, what's going on? The president is wondering what the aliens are going to do.

Sarah texted back: I'm in contact with RAW Charles. What did they tell you?

Charles, the defense secretary texted back: The Pentagon knows what they're doing with the man in Iceland. The United States is not to blame.

Sarah texted back: He's at the naval base in Keflavik. What do you mean the United States is not to blame?

Charles texted back: The man is trying to crack the Chinese military encryption that launches their missiles. He is acting on his own behalf.

Sarah texted back: How do I know that the NSA is not forcing him to do that? Can you communicate with him or pinpoint his location?

Charles texted back: That would be a volatile condition because his life would be at risk Sarah. Sorry I have to go.

Chapter 10

One of the aliens appeared at the India Consulate and confronted Ravi. "Our primary focus of our extraterrestrial mission is India on this planet Earth Ravi. The man is Hindu and he is obliged to serve Lord Krishna which in our case is Anthony. The Muslims and Christians have a false religion because they resist the sexuality of the woman. In our world a woman is the master and men have no problem with that unlike here on Earth. We know the sexuality of the spirit is being suppressed by those in authority with their education system. They don't want Amar or Anthony to know about her and this is a crime of negligence. They are involved with her in love using God. They use her to learn in school especially in college and to make work easy for them. The ones who are creating a problem are the ones you see talking a lot. When Anthony's or Amar's mentality is null they use that as an excuse to harm with force. Those who claim to know what's going on are threatened by hospitalization in the psychiatric hospital. The economic system and the police are perpetuating this evil system and these entities are controlled by those in government."

"Let me make no mistake about it alien, I do believe that women should have authority over man. My parents taught me that and I have no reason to believe otherwise," said Ravi. "India is not null about this Alien and the politics favor the authority of woman, even in our religion Hinduism. What is your point, I would like to know?"

"I was just trying to test what your conviction was, and in this case you have passed my test. I am honored Ravi that you trust me. You are a very humane person and I do recognize that with my heart. Since our people were abused long ago, I give reverence to the few of you who are like that on this planet Earth. Please take this gem as a gift as a token of my respect for you," said the alien. The alien reached inside a bag taken from inside his clothing and passed the stone to Ravi. Ravi looked at it with much interest in his hand and placed it on his desk. "Sharon, have this stone placed in the Dr. Bhau Daji Lad Museum. That museum is in Mumbai alien and I hope you don't mind me making everyone view it."

Sharon said, "Ravi, I will call the Courier and make that arrangement." She has a broad and pleasant smile on her face. "Here is a glass of apple juice with ice unexpected visitor," said Sharon.

"Thank you miss, that was very kind of you," said the alien with a gentle and understanding smile. "The Hindu sociology has kept its foundation for thousands of years and that is very admirable."

"Has your world faced war like here on Earth?" Asked Sharon.

The alien said, "Yes. there were great forces disguised as Gods but they were not. They killed many of our people but our technology finally defeated them. Now we are faced with the Antichrist and the outcome of that is uncertain. A large part of our decisions will be determined by the reasoning of Anthony. Our race is not better than the human beings on Earth for dealing with human matters. Let me project a hologram so you can see our world. Look! What do you think of that image. Wait, let me lower the spectrum of light for your world. There.

"Wow, beautiful. A sphere like here on Earth. The orange color makes me think of Holiness in India. That would explain the irony why you are here at the Indian Consulate. Is my conclusion true?" Said Sharon

We are in the future and past and control the fate of the entire universe so we have to maintain a high integrity of living.

Some of us engage in chanting Hindu hymns so as to the regards of your question, you are correct." Said the alien. "We would love to take you to our world. I think you would find it very enticing Sharon. The males of our species would find you very stimulating and I know this because we have many similar qualities. Also we love okra and shrimps with roti and as in India, tea is our favorite beverage. You will even see the Hibiscus growing in our world and I point that out because I know it is related to Hinduism."

Ring; ring; ring...A call was coming in on her desk phone. "Hello India consulate. Sharon speaking…"

"Sharon this is Sarah from the FBI. How are you doing today?"

"I'm doing fine Sara. How are you?"

"I'm in my home in Harlem calling you. I'm supposed to give Kismet a call about what is going on with the man in Reykjavik. What is his personality like?"

"He's a very conscientious person and he is reserved in his opinions because he values the views of others. He doesn't believe in violence. He uses reason with patience to resolve his psychological conflicts and like most Hindus he doesn't eat beef since the cow is sacred. British colonialism was something very solemn to him and he regrets that so many Hindus died because of conflicts with Muslims." Said Sharon.

"Where did he go to school and what was his occupation Sharon?" Said Sarah.

"I thought you have this information Sarah, I mean you're from the FBI?"

"Sharon just bare with me. Just please answer the question."

"Okay. Okay Sarah. He studied law at the University of London and his job was a lawyer for the Tata group. He found out that Tata was funding Al-Qaeda then Tata fired him saying that it was a lie. He believed that Al-Qaeda was developed by the Americans in order for Jews to have more of a claim to Israel. You don't have to believe me but what do you think?"

"I'd like to know what Anthony's doing aboard the alien ship. In fact I'm going to call Amar before I call Kismet to see what I can say to her." Sarah made an international call to Amar who is in Iceland right now.

Ring.....Ring.....Ring..... "Hello, good evening, this is Amar. Who is this?"

"Amar this is Sarah from the FBI, what's going on?"

"Wait let me raise my volume some, okay. What's going on Sara? Prem said you were going to call Kismet to update her on the man. What did you find out Sarah?"

"I have to be introverted and think like a detective Amar in order to find a solution that I believe is useful. Actually I'd like to know about your paranoia and what you concluded with it that explains reality in this case."

"Well it's like this Sara. The subversion is because they are thinking with numbers and we can't decode that with our brains. Then they mathematically square the intelligence to create time to control the physical with time. Because of this the spirit cannot pass through the material or time and that is why we don't know what's going on beyond our present environment without communication of an electronic nature. The spirit cannot see through itself and the blood is stopping it to the conscience. I'm saying that the man has a similar problem as we have given that criteria. I can instruct the system to prevent them from squaring the Intelligence on a local basis since a scope beyond is hard to fathom." Said Amar.

"What do you do if God is causing this squaring of the intelligence?" Said Sarah.

"Well Sarah, that is why Anthony is going to Canis Major. My Emissary Cnatla will be accompanying Anthony and she is in full control of the system. Call Kismet and update her, okay? Bye.

Sarah was in apprehension, not sure what she had to say to Kismet. She knew there could be a conflict with the FBI and RAW and since Kismet works for RAW, she can't be as innocent as she wants to be and that works on her conscience. Anyhow Sarah made up her mind and dialed Kismet.

Kismet's phone rang five times and she answered it. "Hello this is Kismet, who is this?"

"Kismet, this is Sarah from the FBI what's going on in India?"

"The aliens are saying they have to digitize our movements and that we have to follow their patterns to do this. We have to turn and look at them and stop-and-start movement when they do. If we don't follow their instructions we won't meet where we're going on time. The formation of our thoughts must delete the formation of time and the next time. The aliens are saying that the status quo is using the theory of mind into matter via thoughts to control us with the physical manifestations as we apply memories. So they just have to think of rain then it'll rain or thinking of getting $100 then they will get $100 in their wallets. They do this in real-time so it won't be noticed since there's no time difference to develop truth with the lies."

Sara said, "Kismet, they must have used the theory that Amar acquired when he was learning electronics. I understand there is theory to music so they must have taken advantage of that also."

Kismet said, "Sarah, Anthony said he couldn't learn the keyboard for his rap music so I'm thinking the aliens prevented this so the status quo wouldn't be able to control us if he learned this."

"I can now extrapolate that the status quo must be intelligence Kismet. Intelligence is needed to communicate so that is how they are hiding in plain sight, as intelligence. Those with good jobs have intelligence so that would explain the condition that those in control have power and money. A lot of them have gold so they may be using the personification gold to control those with fascination to understand this spirit. If they are intelligence, why would someone want to learn to be a doctor or a teacher or a scientist? Those who created the pyramids in Egypt must be the ones responsible for the damage of society because the pyramids are mathematical in nature," said Sarah.

Kismet said, "Sarah it is clear that intelligence is the enemy to me and it seems we have to be wrong to defy the right so we can control the intelligence in a non-destructive fashion. So if 2 - 3 equal 7, how do we apply that in life? Wouldn't this mean we have to stop time to see the logic?"

"That is why I am suspicious of truth Kismet, intelligence relies on truth to keep order. The aliens are hesitant to appear on Earth because they would be governed by the truth and their feelings would be jeopardized by this."

"I can now conclude that intelligence must have been forcing the man to develop the truth with his movements so their conspiracy can keep functioning," said Kismet. "Sarah, Amar's Emissary Cnatla is speaking on TV right now. Do you have a TV right now there in America to look at right now?"

"Yes, let me go in the living room and turn on the TV Kismet." Sarah walked fast to her living room. She reached for the push button switch and turned on her Toshiba digital television. "I see her on channel 2 Kismet. She's saying that the aliens are here for their eyes. It appears that the humans have the eyes of the aliens and that the aliens must recover those eyes."

Cnatla continued: "God and his angels have taken the eyes of the aliens and placed it under control in the human beings. The eyes are used to see the lies which is invisible to the human beings. The human beings are really seeing reality with their minds. It is the objective of the aliens to recover those eyes so they can see the lie and correct the problem of this world that has remained unknown. Governments around the world have been collaborating with the Antichrist to keep the function of the eyes unknown. It is my responsibility as system Emissary to provide all required assistance to the aliens so that their objectives will become manifested. They have indicated that copies or duplicates of the eyes that the humans have can be placed in them when they are removed and this can be done painlessly with transmutation."

Sae from the lead alien ship began to speak.

Sae said, "We have learned a lot from the secrets of this world humans. Theory is in the body as the muscle of God and that is why mathematics cannot be understood. Scientific physical constants are set by the cross of Jesus and we have to undo that by recovering the cross. I know those of you who are responsible are monitoring us right now-you are warned to surrender it immediately. For the sake of Jesus we are prepared to destroy all of you if our desires are not met."

The leader Vorlon began to speak...

"Our mission in this world is honorable and any attempt to defy us will be futile. We are consolidating our mission automatically right now with the function of your body and mind and attempts to circumvent that will only be automatically corrected in the action of life. If by any chance we do fail in our mission your own electronics technology will engage automatically and complete the process with a catastrophic level of destruction. I know you don't want that so please cooperate."

End of transmission came on the screen.

Sara said to Kismet, "Under this tranquility of life things are quite serious Kismet."

"It is clear Sara that God is the enemy and must be stopped. The cover of religions has really made him appear innocent. I still have belief in Krishna but I will not think of him as God."

Meanwhile in Iceland Amar and Shanta were trying to develop a plan to intercept the man. There was a low-frequency being received which suggests that he was being transported in a helicopter from Keflavik to where he was going and this was occurring at least once every 3 days. If a gyroscope in his beacon is vibrating we can determine the fundamental pattern of his movement and locate him with a burst of electromagnetic energy. They decided to use a magnetron from a microwave oven and direct the energy of pulses in the area of possible location with a drone. "I'm going to ask Sae from the alien ship if they can assemble the required drone and the required electronic circuitry to scan the area," said Shanta.

"Cnatla, can you open communications to Sae," said Amar.

"Hello Amar this is Sae, what do you request?"

"My sister Shanta would like to talk to you about requesting a drone to locate the man. There is a beacon being transmitted from him and we believe the US military is keeping him hostage," said Amar.

Shanta said, "We need a pulsed magnetron sent to the source of the beacon and check for the resulting feedback signal so we can locate where the beacon is being monitored. The scanning can be done with the drone. Can you provide one?"

"Shanta there's a risk that the alien technology can be stolen. It is best that you use human technology and I think the Russians can provide the drone that is cloked so the Americans would not see it. Allow me to contact the Russian defense minister Sergey Shoygu and let's see if he can provide a drone for us." Sae created a telephone link from the ship's computer to the defense minister's office. The defense Minister's secretary picked up the call and said:

"Defense Minister's office, how may I help you?"

"This is Sae from the lead alien ship. I would like to speak to the defense minister."

"Mr. Shoygu, please pick up the phone on line one," the secretary yelled.

"Defense minister here, how may I help you?"

"This is Sae from the alien fleet. I am requesting a drone because we need to locate the man. We have cloaking technology so we will remain undiscovered."

"What capabilities do you need the drone to do Sae," said the Russian defense minister.

"Defense minister, basically I need radar from a pulsed magnetron emitter aimed at the area where the man may be so we can pinpoint his location to retrieve him. Can you provide a drone with that requirement?" Said Sae

"We would have to do some simple modification but yes, yes Sae, the answer is yes. It would have to be secretive because of the U.S. naval base at Keflavik. Are you saying that America is holding the man against his will Sae?"

"We would have to locate him to be sure defense minister." Said Sae.

"Send a drone immediately defense minister and upon it's arrival near Iceland we will cloak it using one of our ships capabilities. Don't worry your pilots will be safe. By the way, how is your president Mr. Vladimir Putin?"

"He's doing fine Sae. He's trying to work out some issues with Venezuela. You know Nicolas Maduro is a fine man but the State Department would want us to believe otherwise. We think your American president is sending aid to control the logistics of Venezuela."

"We are on shaky ground here Mr. defense minister and we are trying to understand the underlying conspiracy to know what medium evil is operating from. We all have to regard the truth and the truth itself may be the deception so the foundation of reality has to be questioned. It appears we all want to be fair but in the process of reaching a conclusion things can get very disturbing with different personalities. We are awaiting the drone sir and have a nice day." Sae said.

Sae informed Shanta that the Russian defense minister was sending the drone and they were standing by for it's entry into the airspace of Iceland. Amar was noticeably happy about the news and gave Shanta a hug and a kiss on her cheek. "The system should know when the drone arrives Shanta so we needn't worry." Amar made an instruction to the system by touching his right hand fingers on his left palm..."System when the drone arrives please cloke it if it isn't already and let me know." Amar then touched his index finger on his left palm saying 'Impulse,' and then closed the instruction with the repetition of the right hand fingers on the left palm. This gesture was done when making an instruction so that the system will not carry out instructions that are not intended, for instance when Amar talks to himself.

Chapter 11

In Earth orbit the captain Vorlon was about to depart for Canis Major with Cnatla and Anthony on board. "It looks like it's time for our journey to begin Anthony," said the Emissary of the system.

"I am glad to have you by my side Emissary. I am truly confident as to your capabilities, especially when making decisions with a given criteria. What year did Amar instruct the system to create you?" Said Anthony.

"That would be 1982 after he was discharged from Montefiore Medical Center which was his first hospitalization on a psychiatric ward. He always was concerned if he did the right thing by creating me knowing that I would have a difficult time. I want you to know that I am very glad to do this job for the sake of the universe-in fact I am honored that he made the system create me. It was not a mistake especially knowing we have made significant progress for human life and other life forms like the aliens."

"What do you like about your creator Amar the most Emissary Cnatla?"

"I like his personality that has been created due to his mental illness and its applications on imagination that has finally bridged to reality," said the Emissary. "He has sustained his beliefs regardless of the enemy not showing any evidence of existence. He does not consider himself power hungry but has remained neutral in his objective to resolve the problems of the universe. On his part

I personally think that this was good discipline. I only wish he finds me a man. How about you Anthony, what do you think of me and you?"

"I hate to disappoint you Emissary Cnatla, but I think you're too young for me. I'm sure with your intelligence and beauty that you will have much admiration from the male gender. There is time Cnatla, please don't worry about that."

There was a look on Cnatla's face that she felt rejected but somehow retained her composure with a dull grimace on her face. "Well I did make an effort Anthony and I thank you for being honest with me. I noticed that you have a lot of empathy for people and I'm sure a long and interesting story can be conceived about that quality."

Sae and Vorlon came into the room where Anthony and Cnatla were. "We have departed Earth orbit. At 5.7 * 10^12 times the speed of light velocity we should take 4 days to get to Canis Major Emissary," said Vorlon. "How do you feel about leaving your home Anthony?"

"I'm sure you have the best intentions sir and I would like you to know that I do trust you. Sae what would be our first directive as we arrive?" Said Anthony.

"Well Anthony, I'm certain God will try to stop us from approaching v y Canis majoris. That star must be the source of pleasure from love for God but who knows I could be wrong and we may discover other conclusions. Our plan is to investigate the star Sirius first to see if the brightest star has significance being the brightest as curiosity and logic would imply."

Meanwhile in Iceland Amar was having an anxiety attack. Shanta suggested that he breathe regularly because she noticed that his breathing has stopped and she concluded that it was due to fear. "I think people don't want to respond to my reactions automatically and instinctively," he told Shanta. "It must be because they don't want me to have any power so as to be the man. I don't think they want me to make any decisions for IT." For instance, those people walking by he said hello to didn't say hello back but acted like they weren't listening. I think it's because they don't want to play with the spirit like children play. When they don't play a transfiguration of the physical does not occur with each other inhibiting the spirit from passing through the material forms as IT tries to think. He figured this was because they (Truth) wanted us to follow unwritten rules of behavior which is based on restrictions to using IT (the spirit).

People can believe whatever they want about other people's behavior but there remains a perpetual continuation of life for whatever purpose to achieve an unknown end. If the end was known the ambition to achieve success would be less, much less. Amar has a purpose because he believes love is causing his mental illness. Being passive made the enemy able to continue their conspiracy because the system copied that inhibition and did not respond physically in life to change things for the better with Amar's knowledge. This was to make him delusional and alienate him from his own system.

It was about 8 pm at night and Amar could now have his 8 pm cigarette. He remembered he took his psychotropics at 7:00 pm, so he went outside in the clear starry night to have his cigarette. This was his reward for reasoning about the unknown to him and he knew the sentient ones (clouds) could relate with him with the smoke from the cigarette. Sometimes he would call the sentient ones "evil ones" with a good connotation probably because of thunder, wind and rain. He has great respect and admiration for the evil ones and promised to himself by promising to them looking at the sky that he is doing this mission for them. A mission to uncover the secrets and enable the evil ones.

The aliens were recovering their eyes from the human beings and creating duplicates for the humans. They were moving in logical order so their movements can be structured and understood. All of this was seemingly subconscious so their lives would not be disrupted.

"Shanta I think the Mexicans may be the evil ones in the body that I see around me." Said Amar. "I noticed that their heads are flat on the back like they fell on the road like I did. Why would they be trying to cross the American border into Texas or Arizona. Is Donald Trump the Antichrist? Why would he be trying to stop them with a border wall? To me it seems like the Mexicans are trying to fulfill or avoid prophesy."

"Maybe their movements control all of us just like the clouds make us move to shelter," Shanta said. "There's a state called New Mexico next to Mexico and maybe it has to be fulfilled that America will become the New Mexico with Mexicans everywhere. So they have to establish homes here for the evil ones in the flesh. Somehow the Antichrist knows this and is directing Donald Trump to build a wall to avoid this. Americans don't want to work and the Mexicans are telling the Americans they want work so the Americans will have work for the spirit under the control of the spirit. The evidence here is that the Mexicans do the hard labor the Americans don't want to touch since they have the education to make the money with easy jobs."

Prem told Amar and Shanta that they should sleep now and await the drone tomorrow. Shanta took some ice cream from the fridge and after eating it she said good night and went to bed so as not to disappoint Prem. Amar had coffee and went to bed. Prem said goodnight to the two of them and also went to bed saying thank you, that it was a good decision they made.

Chapter 12

Arrival at Sirius.

Captain Vorlon's ship arrived at Sirius and it started scanning for intelligent life such as brain activity. Sirius is the brightest star seen from Earth and there must be a reason why. This star is associated with the Egyptian god Osiris related to agriculture. Yudhistira, a prince of India was followed by this dog star, Svana.

"What are the scanners showing?" said captain Vorlon.

"The system has detected a heartbeat of 150 with a respiration of 100." Said the science officer. "Electrical impulses indicate an animal with four feet, which could be a dog. Checking, Checking. Confirmed, spectrogram images indicates that it is a dog. The dog appears to be existing in a state of fusion within the star Sirius."

"How can we remove the dog from the star Sirius science officer," said captain Vorlon.

"We have to remove the hydrogen from that area and then remove the dog when it's in the state of helium before carbon Fusion starts." Said the science officer.

"Okay do that science officer," said Captain Vorlon.

"Pinpoint the location of the dog signature and remove the hydrogen from the inside and put it on the outside of the star with the graviton controller engineer," said the science officer.

"Initializing hydrogen extraction now," said the engineer.

"The star is increasing in brightness engineer, you must stop the hydrogen extraction, a supernova will occur," said Cnatla.

"A supernova will occur captain Vorlon, stopping hydrogen extraction process," said the engineer.

"The dog could be the man's dog, we have to ask the man to use his heart computer to save the dog. There must be a Fail-Safe that only the man can unlock," said Cnatla.

After agreeing to listen to Cnatla, the crew then left Sirius and continued to Canis majoris.

Chapter 13

The system was scanning the airspace and noticed that the drone was arriving in Icelandic air space. The system sent an automated message to the drone at an aircraft frequency determined to be 5.5 megahertz, "This is system control, please identify yourself?"

"System this is a Russian drone that was requested, please cloak us immediately."

"What is the password that was given to you Russian drone?"

"The password is volcanic 35."

The system noted that this was a correct password and cloaked the drone and requested that the drone pilot land on an island east of Iceland. Operational plans would be given in the morning.

"Thank you system, request confirmed, initiating landing," the pilot radioed.

This was good news. In the morning the system will notify Amar and Shanta that the drone to locate the man was here. Since the Emissary Cnatla was awake, the system informed her that the drone was there off Iceland. Anthony was visibly glad to hear the news from Cnatla. "Amar and Shanta should be very happy when they wake up Emissary," he said. "What kind of signal will the magnetron send to the man's beacon Emissary?" Said Anthony.

Sae said, "I also would like to know your thought on this Emissary."

"Basically we will send signals at certain frequencies to check for a beat frequency of the beacon to understand the current flow in it to understand if it is the man's physiology of movement compared to his stress test records that we have." Said Cnatla.

"Why is the man so important Emissary?" Sae asked.

"Well Sae, a long time ago humans had paranormal capabilities but they were removed by God because God wanted love and that love took the spirit of Krishna and rendered him disabled. In order to create life, the spirits had to make a reference human being that was vulnerable to emotions, feelings and pain and emotional love. This person had to be conceived by a woman through intercourse and given birth and allowed to grow naturally so as to set a foundation which was indestructible for human life. This foundation of life assisted in the redevelopment of Krishna according to our beliefs and this is why Anthony's here alive and well. Anthony represents the Jesus Christ that was crucified and will enable the stopping and reversal of time so that the healing process will manifest. If it was not for the sacrifice of the man Anthony would have no way of being on Earth.

"Anyone for some California wine? I made sure I got some from Earth before we left," said Vorlon. "I heard the Cabernet type is very robust and enjoyable. Please each of you take a glass and let me pour some for you. Add some ice from the bucket."

"Excellent idea Vorlon," said Anthony. "The sedation of this will definitely calm my nerves. Emm. I feel the tranquility of this almost immediately. My psychotropics has created a small high in combination with the wine. I have to limit my intake so my sensibilities are not eroded."

Cnatla asked Vorlon, "Vorlon you have a female companion? I'm curious to know how it works in your world. Please intrigue us."

"Cnatla my dear Emissary, we have complementary mates just like on Earth. Offsprings are produced through an energy interface unlike the physical sex act. A transaction of emotion develops the child due to ecstasy energy similar to an orgasm of humans but may last much longer-minutes. The child is formed in a capsule remotely and not in the female body."

A beautiful sunrise was arising in Iceland and the alarm clock woke up Shanta. Shanta went to Amar's room and woke him up. "Shanta what's the..."

"They already brought us breakfast." Said Shanta. "It's bacon and eggs with toast. Make coffee the usual way, two sugars and milk?"

"Two sugars and milk is fine Shanta. Do you like the breakfast?" Said Amar.

"It looks great. Why wouldn't I like it Amar? I can make my own decisions right?"

"Judgment is a good gift and making your own decisions from how you feel Shanta. Those in control would wish that we didn't have those freedoms."

"There is a message on my phone that the drone has arrived Amar. The message came from Cnatla. It says the system has initiated drone scanning in the area for the man." Said Shanta.

"Tell Cnatla to check for not-so-obvious indicators such as the clear density in the transparency of the air. This may identify unknown intelligences in the area that are undergoing covert operations." Said Amar.

"Amar I sent the message and Cnatla replied that the Russians are aware of this. She wants to know who manufactured the beacon." Said Shanta.

"Tell her that these beacons are usually known to be made in East Germany. It could have even been made in Scandinavia, possibly Norway. Tell her we will contact the Russians for that information."

Shanta said, "Done Amar!"

Amar used his cell phone and called Sarah from the FBI.

Ring...Ring...."Hello; Sarah speaking?"

"Hello Sarah, good morning how are you?"

"It's so nice to hear your voice Amar. What do you need?"

"Sara, how are Anthony's parents in the Bronx?"

"They're concerned about their son but they have confidence in the aliens. What are you doing right now Amar. I mean how is it in Iceland?"

"Iceland is great, the weather is warm and the humidity is excellent," said Amar. I want to know what frequency the CIA uses on the spy beacons for personnel. Do you have that information Sarah?"

"Amar I think they operate at 2 gigahertz. There's a pulse every 12 seconds and I think they're the size of a cigarette lighter. Is this in reference to the man?"

"I guess the Russians would know that information about the beacon right? So they should know how to scan for the man, am I right again?" Said Amar.

"What are they scanning with?"

"They're using a magnetron to develop microwaves."

"In receiving mode the magnetron should detect the beacon Amar. Just scan between 2 to 3 gigahertz."

"The KGB is on the phone Amar," said Shanta.

"Sarah let me please put you on hold. I have to talk to the KGB. Hello this is Amar speaking..."

"Hello Amar, this is Anatoly from the KGB. We need the man's EKG trace, can you provide it?"

"Yes Anatoly, I have the man's EKG on my laptop as a PDF. I can email it to you. What is your email address?"

Anatoly told Amar, "ay35kgb@gmail.com. Please send it as soon as possible. We have to confirm that we have detected the man."

Amar quickly got his laptop and powered it on and connected to the Wi-Fi. He then emailed the EKG file of the man to Anatoly.

"Anatoly since you're still on the line, my Emissary would like to know who manufactures the beacon?" Said Amar

"Amar, the beacons are manufactured by Sinetron in East Germany. The United States military has a contract with them." Said Anatoly.

After Anatoly got the email he radioed ahead to the drone pilot a fax so they could compare the EKG to the magnetron scanner. The beacon was transmitting a signal comparable to the EKG pulse rate pattern and amplitude so they could say they had a confirmation to the man. There was however an anomaly. The beacon was pulsing every 10 seconds instead of 12 seconds and was non-existent for 30 second periods and it was traveling between 15 to 30 miles an hour.

Anatoly sent a text to Amar saying that the man may be in a submarine on the surface and was diving for 30 second periods and this will account for no signal because submarines cannot send radio signals underwater for long distances. They must have adjusted the pulse rate to identify the man and to deviate the source of the signal. He sent a signal to one of the KGB spy satellites to take a photo of the coordinates of the signal. The satellite sent a signal back to the drone and surprisingly upon his observation it appeared to be a submarine. Immediately he contacted the Russian Navy and requested that they intercept the submarine. He inquired to Amar asking him why would the Americans be holding the man in a submarine.

Amar called Sarah from the FBI and asked her, "Sara, this is Amar. We believe the man is in a submarine off Iceland Sara. Can you find out why he's there?"

"So he's not in a helicopter?" Said Sara.

"I think he may have been shuttled in a helicopter also Sarah," said Amar.

"Amar, let me contact the defense secretary again, maybe he knows more than he made me believe." Said Sarah, "I'll call you soon. Goodbye."

Sarah dialed the number for the defense secretary at the Pentagon.

Ring...Ring. Ring...

"Defense secretary, who may I have the honor of speaking with?"

"Charles this is Sarah. Things have gotten a little more interesting concerning the man. We know he's in a submarine off

Iceland. My question to you is why would he be in a submarine and what is he doing there?"

"Sarah why don't you rescue him if you think he's being held against his will?"

"That's part two of my question, how do I rescue him?"

"First of all Sarah you should find out why the man is really there instead of jumping to conclusions that he is in danger. I've just heard from sources that a Russian Navy fleet is in the area and would attempt to rescue him. Tampering with the American military at Keflavik can create a world war."

"Charles we're talking about the man that defied God. I would risk anything to rescue him. If it wasn't for the man we would all be dead by now, don't you agree?"

"I understand you know Kismet from the Indian intelligence RAW agency. The man is of Indian-origin, I'm sure Kismet knows what to do. Have a talk with her Sarah," said Charles.

"Forgive me for my cynicism Charles. I just want you to have a good day and please ignore my temperament. As soon as I hang up I will contact Kismet. How's your wife and three kids?"

"We're doing fine here in DC. The weather is nice today and tonight we might go see the latest Avengers movie. How was your day Sarah? You seem to carry a lot of anxiety but I respect your effort to resolve problems."

"Yes Charles I am stressed but I'm doing things for the greater good. Maybe tonight I'll have a glass of wine. Jesus means everything to me. You have a good night Charles.. goodbye."

"Good night baby," said Charles.

Sarah dialed Kismet's number and after a delay of 7 rings Kismet answered her phone. "Hi Sarah. I know it's you because of the caller ID. What's up?"

"Well Kismet they're using the man for the truth and I got to figure out a way to understand how that process is going on. The Russians are converging on the submarine that he is in. Can you tell me anything that I should be aware of?" said Sarah

"Surprisingly in this short time Sarah, the Russians have boarded the submarine according to RAW intelligence. I just got a report that they have apprehended the captain of the ship and have taken the man on board their Navy vessel. The Americans did not retaliate with weapons because four Russian Navy ships had a weapons lock on the American submarine. Apparently they didn't care if the man was killed. The Russians must have been bluffing. Anyhow they're questioning the man right now according to their transmissions to Indian intelligence. You don't need to worry Sarah, you just chill. The system is applying auto correction functionality of human life," said Kismet to Sara. "There's a safe area buffer to prevent harm to the human body."

Chapter 14

At Captain Vorlon's ship

Aboard the alien ship Sae was looking out the window at the constellations. "Life is mysterious yet beautiful Anthony," Sae said. "Clusters of stars show that the work of Krishna was not finished on time. What were you not able to finish Anthony?" Sae said.

"My subconscious is telling me an idea Sae, I was not able to finish an idea. An idea to create a difference with my idea. But that is reasoning with the truth and the truth is false. The Antichrist has taken my energy and I have little or no energy. I don't know what's powering them but they don't want me to have any power. There will be a solution when I change those who cannot be changed Sae. They have to heed my warning."

"I am looking at the constellation Pisces Anthony, it is up and to your left. I noticed you're very sensitive and that's the way Pisces people are. There is definitely truth to astrology. I can recognize Orion, do you recognize Orion?"

"I do recognize Orion Sae. To the south of it is Canis Major, our destination," said Anthony. "I'm wondering who betrayed Lord Krishna that caused the destruction of the universe. It must have been someone he loves because he couldn't harm any life to correct this devastation. I am glad the man allowed us to live despite the tragedy caused by God. You would think that Krishna is infallible Sae but apparently I am not."

Meanwhile aboard the Russian Navy vessel the man was being questioned about his treatment and purpose aboard the American submarine. The man looks physically fit and healthy but psychologically he was degraded according to the ship's psychiatrist. Doctor Baryshnikov noted that the man's mind was erratic because of the movement of his eyes. The man was curious and inquisitive about what was happening to him but couldn't prove anything and nothing was explained to him by the Americans. The doctor prescribed him the antidepressant Luvox to serve as a tranquilizer so he would get some much needed sleep and reassured him that he was safe aboard that Russian Navy vessel. "What is your name man?" The doctor asked.

"My name is Vijay, thank you for helping me and rescuing me from the Americans. Lucifer is controlling my decisions and I need to know where the automotive switch is because I have to activate my heart computer."

Doctor Baryshnikov said, "Vijay for now please try to relax. I want your mind to be clear so you can make good decisions and when you improve we will try to find the switch for you, O.K.?"

"When I activate the heart computer it is then that I would be able to make better decisions doctor. Time is crucial, you must let me have access to the switch. The aliens need me to have the power to stop love because the universe keeps expanding."

"OK Vijay, I know who has the switch and I'm going to contact them now." Said Dr. Baryshnikov.

Earlier Sarah did contact the captain of the Navy ship and told him that Amar has the switch for the man and that is how Dr. Baryshnikov knew. Sarah was at risk of being charged with espionage so she took a great chance in informing the Russians. Sarah made a phone call to Amar that the man was rescued and that Amar could deliver the switch to him after learning from the Russian Navy that the man was in their custody.

Dr. Baryshnikov told Vijay that he was going to talk to the captain to inquire about the switch and how it can be delivered to the Navy ship. "Vijay you must excuse me for a few minutes, I'm going to talk to the captain."

He went down a narrow passageway between two bulkheads and took the elevator up to the bridge. There the captain was enjoying a Rothmans cigarette and a cup of Café Bustelo coffee. "How are you doing doctor. How is our guest?

"He has mild trauma but he's fine. How are we going to deliver the switch to the man?" Doctor Baryshnikov asked the captain.

"We will soon arrive at the Reykjavik port and from there we are going to call Amar and ask him to deliver the switch. In fact I will call him now with my phone." The captain said.

After the captain finished his cigarette he dialed his phone and after 9 seconds Amar picked up his phone. "This is Amar, who may I have the pleasure of speaking with?"

"Amar this is Captain Ivan of the Navy vessel Sophia, how are you?"

"I'm good captain. I want to deliver the switch to the man and I understand you have him on your ship?"

"That is what I was calling about Amar, we will reach the port of Reykjavik in 5 hours with our current speed and I'm wondering if you can rendezvous with us there?"

"I fear that the American Navy is at that port and you will have trouble upon entry," said Amar.

"Amar, our battlegroup is approaching that area, we have submarines and battleships and destroyers heading for that port." Ivan said. "Amar, where are you exactly? I want to send a helicopter to shuttle you over here to one of our carriers."

Amar said, "I can be at Klambratún park at 2pm today. I will be with two other persons, my sister and someone from R&AW of Indian intelligence. I will be walking with the switch for the man so make sure you have high security. Ivan, there has been two men following me around and I think they're from the

Icelandic police and I think their intention is to protect me, possibly from the American intelligence."

"Amar, I suspect it is because of the switch. The Icelandic police don't want the Americans to prevent you from giving it to the man since the man can control the computers with the interface of his heart computer," said Ivan. "Don't worry Amar, we have your best interests in mind and also the aliens are there to protect you although it is not that obvious to you. Expect the helicopter to arrive shortly to pick you up and your guests."

A Jeep approached them and 2 American soldiers got off and confronted them. "I'm Sergeant McGregor, why are you here?"

Amar answered, "Do you see that spaceship approaching sergeant? We are here to meet the aliens."

The sergeant replied, "I have orders from my commander that the three of you are not allowed to interact with aliens. Furthermore if you all do not leave immediately I will be forced to arrest you all."

The alien craft made a landing and distracted the military personnel. "Officers, drop your weapons or we will be forced to engage ours," echoed from the spaceship. At that time the helicopter was approaching and proceeded to land. Two military officers got off and walked towards Amar and the others. The Soviet officers knew they were safe from the American military because of the spaceship.

"What are we going to do now," said one American military officer to the other. The other officer said, "We are going to leave but before we leave I want to inform you all that you are against American policies and we consider this a threat to national security."

Prem couldn't help but say, "Our intention is to do what is morally correct and our jurisdiction here defines that purpose so we are immune from any kind of charges that you may consider legally binding."

"Leave here immediately! You will be doing your country a favor," said Shanta to the military officers.

As everybody was noticing each other the two men that were following them approached and it was the Icelandic police. One of them spoke to the three, "I understand Amar that you have the switch for the man and as such it is our prerogative to have the American soldiers depart peacefully otherwise the aliens in that spaceship you see, will open fire. Do you want that gentleman," the taller Icelandic policeman told the shorter American military personnel.

Suddenly in a quick and shocking move both American soldiers rushed the Icelandic policemen and grabbed them by the throat with their weapons drawn. "Hand over the switch Amar or I will kill these officers!" said the taller American soldier.

In their trepidation an alien emerged from the spaceship and slowly walk to their location. The American soldiers fired their weapons at the alien but that did not seem to have any harm inflicted on him. Some type of photon pulses was emitted from the spaceship at the American soldiers and rendered them unconscious. The Icelandic policemen were relieved and struggled to catch their breath from the choke holds. Amar, Shanta, and Prem looked at each other in amazement and wondered what type of capability the alien had with him. "Get on the helicopter the three of you and let the Russians take you to the man aboard their Russian ship," Said the alien who was now a couple of feet away from them. "What is in your attaché," Said the alien to Amar.

"I have the switch for the man and the power supply in the attaché, plus a laptop for him," Said Amar to the alien and the three of them rushed off to the waiting helicopter.

The Russian soldier in the helicopter reached out his hand and helped the three of them on board. "Come on get on board quickly. Chinese and American jet fighters are approaching. We will be safer when we're airborne."

The alien went in the spaceship and lifted off and hovered above the area where the helicopter was leaving so as to protect it from anticipated jet fired missiles.

"How are you doing," said Captain Ivan from the Sophia to the helicopter pilot over the radio.

"Captain we're airborne and will arrive in 10 minutes." Said the helicopter pilot. "I just deployed a flare because there was a missile that just passed me. It appears that the alien ship just put a shield around the helicopter captain Ivan."

"Keep your eyes on your sensors," captain Ivan said. "Our monitors indicate that another missile will intercept you in 5 seconds. Deploy a flare now."

"I don't have time captain," said the helicopter pilot. "I got distracted from the alien ship. Woh, the missile hit the shield and exploded. We're okay. I have them on my monitor. I'm going to turn around and return fire."

The old Mil mi-24 did a 180 turn in a matter of 2.2 seconds and returned fire with two heat seeking rockets at the unidentified aircrafts. They could see in the distance that the missiles acquired the targets and destroyed two aircrafts.

In trepidation Amar, Shanta and Prem were at the mercy of the weapons operator but then showed the sign of excitement at the precision targeting. The Mil mi-24 made another 180 degree turn around and headed for the Soviet ship. "You don't have to cry Shanta, we're fine," Amar said to Shanta as he cradled his left arm around her. Shanta is known for her strong personality but this was a little too much.

I'm sure the aliens had the capabilities to stop the missiles from the US Air Force but it was all part of a test. A test to see the decisions of when mental feelings and physical feelings converge in a person. In order for the aliens to accomplish their mission here on Earth, they have to find out how humans think. As they execute this test, that evaluation will uncover the unknown, especially the classified information that governments have kept secret from their citizens by means of the geometry of information that people contain. This can manifest as confirmation of suspicion due to the words expressed as we think that those words will be expressed at that moment.

As the Soviet fleet was approaching Shanta asked the helicopter pilot if that was the ship they were going to land on she saw as she pointed at it, "Yes my dear we are going down for a landing. I hope you aren't too shook up."

The helicopter descended slowly and touched down with a little shake and finally became stationery on the ship. The wind was blowing rather hard, probably 15 knots or more. Captain Ivan approached the helicopter and welcomed them. "Well I'm glad you're all safe. Do you have the power supply for the switch Amar?"

"I have the power supply Captain but I like to know if you have 120 volts ac on the ship?" Said Amar

"We do Amar, we have 120 volt and 220 volts but at 50 hertz. Will that be okay?" Said captain Ivan

"That should be okay Captain because I don't see why 120 volts at 50 hertz will not work compared to 60 hertz. How is the man, I would like to see him so we can enable the switch?"

"Relax Amar, I want the three of you to have dinner first with the man so we can discuss what concerns we have." Said captain Ivan. "Soldier, take their belongings and take them to their quarters. Dinner will be at 19:00 hours."

Chapter 15

Meanwhile Anthony and Cnatla and the aliens arrived at Canis Major and was orbiting one of the planets around Canis majoris. They started looking for life forms on the planet and the nearby planets orbiting the other stars. "What do we look for?" Cnatla asked Sae. "The star is highly active. What is that all about?"

"It's definitely not at peace, something must be affecting it that we do not see." Said Anthony. "I always wondered how God couldn't disable us if he wanted to at any time."

Commander Vorlon came in the room and also took a look at the star Canis majoris. "Excuse the interruption, I overheard you Anthony. God cannot harm us because he would be losing part of himself if he did."

"And what is that part that he would be losing commander Vorlon, if I may be candid?" Emissary Cnatla uttered.

"He would be losing his belief because we make up part of that belief for one thing." Stated commander Vorlon. "He would be also losing his guilt because he controls us with that guilt we feel and he likes to extend that guilt on us. Another thing is that we control the geometry of his plans by the way we move around and if he loses one of us that would be like losing a piece in the game of chess."

"We believe he is right here so how do we identify him," said Sae to commander Vorlon.

"Well Sae, let's start the reasoning process. He makes us feel his guilt, so what are you observing that can be identified as a source of that guilt?"

"Probably my mistrust of who I am and my intelligence commander," Sae said. "So then I can conclude that God is in my body or mind. And since my mind is in my body, God may be my flesh and all our bodies' flesh. So it must be a deception when he makes us believe that we shouldn't think of the flesh. We cannot kill the flesh otherwise we will die so what can we do commander?" Asked Sae.

"I believe you are correct Sae but what can we do is the question that must be answered," commander Vorlon queried. "Do you know the answer Emissary Cnatla?"

"Commander Vorlon, I think we have to oscillate the mind at a certain frequency to neutralize the flesh control of God. He may be causing Anthony's anxiety attacks like a signal at an antenna point of contact with a wire. It may be in the earth FM band frequency range. The truth has to be controlled, so we have to recreate the lie of the truth. If we can split the body in two safely I think that would do it. There has to be a difference of time for the lie to manifest. We can use the same logic as an FM ratio detector that uses phase and the decoder which separates left and right channels as male and female for stereo. With feeling normal the nerves are conducting love unknowingly. When there is no love for the nerves to conduct, time becomes afraid as well as love itself. This suggests that time and love are as guilty as God, for God lives on love. Love is between mental time and the physical time and that is why we're rushing all the time in confusion trying to accomplish our tasks. Mental time is trying to coincide with physical time. There is a phase difference between mental time and physical time and if we can identify that like an FM ratio detector we would be able to see the two as separate.

Anthony said, "Why don't we simply look in a mirror. Isn't there a phase difference there? The phase difference is 180 degrees and that should be the answer. There is a cancellation of mental time and physical time but we can see the difference in a mirror, the difference of both. Since the image in the mirror is not real, that must represent the mental time. I should also add that God does not want to remember anytime of time because then we will remember the direction of our thoughts and the confusion we have of life would go away. God and his word are not feeling matter, that is why we are disabled and cannot apply force to thought.

Commander Vorlon said, "Since we are dealing with a balanced condition with God we should apply the intermediate frequency of the FM IF (Intermediate frequency) to Canis Majoris which would be 10.7 megacycles. Our dish antenna can point a 10.7 gigahertz harmonic at that frequency to the star. We can start the power of the signal at 100 milliwatts and then increase it to a level that causes a reaction of the star."

Sae said, "I will inform the helm immediately to initiate that process Commander Vorlon." Sae used her communicator to send the message to the helm and the helm replied that they would do it in five minutes. They were all anxious to see it happen and what would be the result.

"We have started the transmission of the fundamental FM 10.7 megacycles carrier to the Canis Majoris star commander Vorlon," said communications officer Valerie. "What are we looking for sir?"

"We are looking for some type of differentiation that would indicate love of God, possibly some type of gender identification." Said commander Vorlon. "I can see there is no reaction occurring so increase the signal to 1 Watt."

"Do you see that Commander," said Sae. "There's a shifting of the colors of Canis majoris indicating there's a heat difference occurring,"

"Okay inject a stereo signal with a 500 Hertz tone on the Left channel and a 1500 Hertz tone on the right channel," said commander Vorlon.

"Part of the star has maintained 3000 degrees Kelvin but another part, about 60%, has reached 9000 degrees Kelvin. This is a 1 to 3 ratio, corresponding with the frequency of the left and right channels of the FM signal," said communications officer Valerie.

"This is a critical stage for the star commander Vorlon, we have to drop the temperature of the star immediately."

"Is the Star resonating with the signal?" Said the Commander.

Canis majoris is resonating at the fifth harmonic or 2500 Hertz of 500 Hertz," said Valerie.

"Lower the frequency of the right channel of the signal to 1000 Hertz," said commander Vorlon. "Status?"

"Resonance has stopped and the star has cooled Commander Vorlon," said Valerie.

Anthony said, "They are using the Hindu 5th Vedas for love Commander."

"Isn't the 5th Vedas a myth Anthony?" Said commander Vorlon.

"Since they are achieving love commander, the 5th Vedas must not be a myth, love must be contained in the 5th Vedas.

"What do you suspect we do now Anthony?" Said commander Vorlon.

"Switch the frequencies of the channels and raise the frequency of the left channel to 1500 hertz." Said Anthony.

"I am doing that right now Commander Vorlon," said communications officer Valerie. "The temperature of the Star is dropping rapidly commander Vorlon and the time continuum is going to be stopped. Fusion temperature of the star has reached critical commander. A black hole will be created. Warning sir,. a black hole will be created; It will pull this part of the universe in along with our ship.

"About 15 asteroids are heading for our ship Sir," said Sae.

"Weapons officer, prepare to fire proton guns at asteroid approaching!" Said commander Vorlon through his communications device.

"The proton guns are not working sir, they cannot reach a ready state, due to time stopping," said the weapons officer. "You have to shut down the FM transmission at the star."

"Please, shut down your signal. I will stop the love," said an image on the communications monitor.

"Are you God?" Said commander Vorlon, directing his attention to the monitor.

"Yes I am God. If I don't feel the love I will feel pain and we'll die. The fifth Vedas has programmed my operations to destroy the universe if I die. It cannot be resetted, it is on automatic."

"This is communications officer Valerie, a transmission is coming from Earth."

"Pipe it to the monitors," said commander Vorlon.

"This is Captain Ivan from the Russian federation ship Sophia. You made us cancel dinner here on Sophia, however I understand the urgency. We are trying to activate the man's heart computer here on Earth. What is your situation with God?"

Commander Vorlon said, "The universe is about to auto destruct because of God's protocol and the 5th Vedas."

Captain Ivan said, "Standby. Give us a few moments, we are setting the current of the failsafe switch to enable the man's heart computer."

"Captain Ivan, hand me the power supply and the ammeter." Said Amar.

Amar adjusted the power supply voltage to 12V and set the current to 100 milliamps. The light of the switch was glowing red. "Man, adjust the gain of the transistor to 120 with your mind and maintain the current flow of 100 milliamps through the collector of the transistor."

"How can I do that Amar, I'm not telepathic," said the man.

"Just concentrate on the spirit man, the spirits will apply the changes on to the circuitry," said Amar.

"My heart computer is sending a message to me," said the man. "It's saying breathe faster. "Now it's saying focus on the switch and think of the HFE (HFE is the gain of the transistor) being 120. I can feel it beating harder now."

The heart computer now says, "This is Data H0, I am now on. Please identify yourself host?"

"This is MAN, identification number 84521."

"Man 84521, authentication established. What is your request," said DATA H0.

"Establish link to the system and Emissary Cnatla in constellation Canis Major." said the man.

"Link established. Emissary Cnatla, what is the problem? This is the Man's heart computer data H0."

Emissary Cnatla rushed speaking and said, "Asteroids will hit this ship in 5 seconds, disable them immediately Data H0."

"Telemetry establishment with system. Now disabling asteroids by redirection. Collision to ship diverted Emissary. The man has indicated there is a problem with God. Can you please explain it?" Said Data H0.

"Data H0, Canis majoris is about to collapse. Can you please prevent that?" Said Emissary Cnatla.

"The man has to communicate with God Emissary. Man, establish communication with God-urgent," spoke Data H0.

"God this is man, differentiate the left and the right so the star will not collapse."

"I can't do that, the love will stop and I will feel pain as a consequence," said God. "You have to give your soul to me man."

"I cannot do that!" said the Man to God.. "I will lose my feelings and will be unable to think for myself."

"Captain Vorlon, I am differentiating the FM signal by oscillating left and right channels so the love will stop." Said Vijay.

Captain Vorlon said, "I can see Canis major equalizing temperatures across itself Man. The love has stopped, thank you Man."

God got very angry and started consuming ethyl alcohol from his belief which made him drunk. He then said, "I'm now launching the Chinese ICBM's to destroy the world."

Seeing that there was no way to stop this, Cnatla requested the man to stop this with the heart computer-to stop the launching of the missiles in China.

Observing this, Amar turned on the man's laptop and gave it to him and Prem inserted the decryption software he had on the flash drive into the laptop. "Open the *Man Configuration* program Vijay and load Prem's software." Said Amar.

"Ten seconds more...Done Amar," Said Vijay. "I am now disabling the launch sequence."

With a link from the laptop to the man's heart computer, in five seconds the laptop responded, "Launch sequence halted, Man's no harm protocol in effect. Do you have further instructions concerning this issue Amar?"

"No DATA H0,"Said Amar relieved.

Disappointed God said, "Man, just give me your soul so I will not use another star for love and then I will return the fifth Vedas 5 to you and Anthony.

"I cannot trust your intelligence. It has been ruling the world forever and has only caused destruction," said man. "You have to enable the mathematics of the physical constants to change values. Change the laws of the universe now or you will be destroyed with Data H0. I would be glad to not worship you knowing you are dead."

"According to Einstein's theory of relativity, every action creates an equal and opposite reaction, so even if you destroy me a new universe and me will be created," said God.

"That's where you're wrong God," said Man, "Matter will be recreated but not intelligence."

"That's where you're wrong Man, intelligence can never be destroyed. Even if you don't sense it it exists in the subconscious and because of that some form of life will detect it." Said God.

Anthony believing he was Krishna queried God by saying, "Who is your Goddess? Why are you without one?"

"I don't need a goddess. I have all your souls to love me. The soul in man and woman is female," blurted God.

"God did you turn the soul of mother Lakshmi into the spirit," said Anthony. "I don't know my girlfriend. Is she in the form of my soul and your soul God?"

"To confirm your doubts Anthony, you are Lord Vishnu and I have committed a crime against you and Man. We conspired for centuries to keep the secret of love which uses the soul. Love stinks so that may give you a clue as to what it is. I ask in return for your soul forgiveness and that I may continue to live if I surrender her. She would be able to eliminate the physical constants of mathematics." Anthony started to dance knowing that God would admire him and be good.

"I guarantee it God, you will survive," Said Anthony.

God went into a trance thinking of the square root of zero to unsquare intelligence and stop time and ejected the soul of mother Lakshmi and some stars were recreated from black holes. Mother Lakshmi quickly went to Anthony's side in horror and joy.

"Oh my dear Krishna, how long has it been; 2,000 years? I'm so glad to be with you. Being with God was a horror," said mother Lakshmi to Anthony.

"What caused my mental illness God and the mental illness of others," said Anthony.

"I crucified you Anthony, you are a reincarnation of Vishnu or Christ. The nails that were in your hands and feet caused mental illness because of the extreme pain. I acquired time with the crucifixion and people were forced to work to survive because of time. You are also seeing with your mind and not your eyes, so you are blind. Angels and people who paid the price of their soul to the devil can see the feeling with their eyes because the eyes can differentiate time since there are two of them in a person."

"So you wanted to keep love a secret," said Commander Vorlon to god. "And you wanted to feel the illusion of grandeur to make life suffer. So you are an illness and Anthony, along with other mentally ill people indirectly suffered from your illness. I can conclude logically that these circumstances can only exist as love for you but you did not want to accept love. I feel great sorrow for you God. What have you lost to do this harm to the human race?"

"I was raped and they took my soul in the process and I wanted revenge so I made the entire human race suffer for this since I felt like nothing. I am sure Commander Vorlon you can understand this," said God.

"Thank you for returning the soul of mother Lakshmi to Anthony God. You will become a human body and be able to coexist among us," said commander Vorlon. Also we need to know the location of the cross of Jesus so we can disable the power of time."

God said, "The cross is located on the planet Jupiter where my servants have been conspiring against life in the universe. Please treat them with mercy. It is my will they were doing and it's not their own, so it is not their fault."

"We are not here to cast judgment God. We know it's your weakness for wanting to feel powerful," said Sae after wiping tears from her eyes. Cnatla also showed elevated empathy with the dialogue.

"I am sending a message to Amar on Earth to go to Jupiter and retrieve the cross of Christ Commander Vorlon," said Cnatla.

"Please send that message Sae," said commander Vorlon. "And also ask the man to retrieve his dog from Canis Majoris."

"The message was received. I'm not waiting for a reply," said Sae.

"This is Amar Emissary Cnatla, we have received your message and will be proceeding to Jupiter as soon as a ship is available. Emissary, we believe the cross of Jesus may be at the center of the eye of the storm on Jupiter. The storm is caused by a temporal distortion because time cannot move in that area. Commander Vorlon can you please authorize a ship on Earth to take us to Jupiter?

"Amar, a ship should be at Iceland in approximately 20 minutes. The ship will notify you when it arrives," said commander Vorlon through Sophia's communications console.

"Shanta, Man your heart computer is working and all three of us will go to Jupiter to retrieve the cross of Jesus," said Amar. "Oh I forgot Prem, you're also going with us."

"DATA H0, remove the dog from Canis Majoris and bring him here to Earth." Said Vijay.

"Ruf, Ruf," the dog barked. "Ruf, Ruf, Ruf," and came to Vijay licking him.

"How are you my friend, it's been so long?" Said Vijay.

"Let's all go have a cigarette," said Shanta. "You do smoke man, don't you?"

"Yes I do Shanta, I do smoke," said the man. "The smoking lifts the emotional weight of Christ off God's belief enabling the change of information of intelligence allowing the physical to transform."

"I've never heard something more brilliant than what you just said man," said Shanta. "So the Antichrist acquired the power of Jesus with the cross?"

"Yes my dear Shanta, the theory was established with the crucifixion of Christ and that same theory can destroy Lucifer. Simply subtract the differences of forces of light levels and we have power over Lucifer," said man. "That is sadly the truth and I'm hoping Anthony would liberate us. I hope Anthony can forgive me for stating the fact so directly."

"I believe with my heart computer in conjunction with the cross of Jesus mother Lakshmi can restore Anthony's mental health," said Vijay. "Commander Vorlon, the ship has arrived and as soon as we board it we will head for Jupiter. Stand by for instructions concerning Anthony and God. As we pass Mars we will stop and try to restore the oxygen there for the aliens."

"Roger Man, the ship Criterion is now requesting that you all get ready for transport onto it. Are all of you ready?" said commander Vorlon.

"Yes we are ready Commander Vorlon, please beam the four of us aboard the ship," said Amar.

Through Sophia's radio the captain of the Criterion, Vax said, "Initializing transport."

The four of them arrived upon the Criterion in a few seconds. Captain Vax said, "Welcome aboard, we are now moving towards Jupiter and will arrive shortly. I understand you have to retrieve a cross there," said Captain Vax to the Man.

We would have to assess the situation according to what we experience there," said Vijay to Captain Vax. "Since my heart computer is functioning, we would have some options available regardless of what the condition is."

"I would like a cup of coffee," said Shanta to captain Vax. "Is that available on this ship captain?"

"I am sure we can accommodate you Shanta. Prem, would you like coffee also? What about you Vijay and Amar?"

All four of them looked at each other and nodded in agreement which the captain visualized as an affirmative response.

"Follow me. Let's take a walk down to our synthesis room," said Vax. "Enter the lift all four of you. We are going down to the third level of the ship. Okay walk this way. Enter here. So far do you like the design of the ship?"

"Very interesting architecture," said the Man. The others were glancing around in amazement as they passed from area to area.

"This is the synthesis room. Whatever you like can be replicated, but of course you must consider its size. This is the model 6402. Ask the synthesizer for the coffee Prem," said Vax.

"Model 6402, 4 cups of coffee please to our taste!" said Prem. "I am assuming it knows our mental characteristics. Okay I'm sorry. Please add one more for Vax."

In 5 seconds the model 6402 prepared the coffee in five porcelain cups according to the taste of the five of them with their names printed on the cups. Everyone was astonished except Vax.

"This coffee is very good. I should try it more often," said Vax. "What do you think of the model 6402 everyone?"

"Excellent reproduction," said Shanta.

"Wonderful. Beyond disbelief," said the man.

The smile on Amar's face was broad and gleeful. "I want to synthesize beer next time," Amar said to captain Vax.

Chapter 16

Mars was quickly approaching. They Criterion carried a large can of chlorophyll to disperse in the Mars atmosphere to turn the co2 into Oxygen. After a minute Mars was below the ship and the Criterion assumed an orbit. They moved to the side of Mars that had sunshine since the chlorophyll had to react with it.

"We have to deploy our chlorophyll payload quickly crew since our objective is Jupiter. Take the ship to five thousand feet from the surface helm," Said captain Vax.

The ship began to lower and declined quickly to five thousand feet. At that point it was to circle Mars and eject the chlorophyll at a steady rate. Captain Vax gave those instructions.

"The ship's computer is indicating that the conversion of the carbon dioxide to oxygen is happening rapidly captain. In one hour the process will complete," said the science officer. "Captain Vax, I want two martians that is on our ship to the go down to test the process conversion."

"Very well then science officer. Prepare the aliens to go down in the shuttlecraft," said Captain Vax.

The aliens went to the loading dock and went into the shuttlecraft. "We're sacrificing ourselves for Anthony, so it's worth it," said one of the aliens.

"I'm sure Anthony doesn't want any sacrifices for himself," said the other Alien.

The cargo bay doors opened and the shuttlecraft descended onto the planet Mars. After 2 minutes of careful maneuvering the pilot landed the shuttlecraft on Mars. "Looks pretty hospitable aliens, go out and check the atmosphere."

"This is our home," said one alien to the other alien, "Let's go out and be brave."

When the hatch opened both aliens went out without any breathing apparatus. Not to our surprise they were both fine with the atmosphere.

"Well we can celebrate, our race can return to Mars!" Said the alien with a smile. You could sense the other alien had a sense of accomplishment.

Both aliens entered the shuttlecraft and returned to the Criterion. Captain Vax was very pleased about the outcome.

The Criterion resumed its journey to Jupiter. I have confidence that with a success on Mars this could mean an easy success on Jupiter.

"Captain Vax, please come to the bridge," said the bridge's navigation officer. "We are approaching Jupiter."

"Okay let's go to the bridge everyone," said captain Vax.

Captain Vax headed for the elevator and they followed him and entered it. He pressed the button for the bridge and in 10 seconds they arrived. He could see Jupiter on the monitor and outside the window.

"Scan to see where time is not passing at the eye of the storm." Said Vax

"There is a small area where different quantities of gases are not interfacing with each other captain," said the science officer. "I am now zooming in on that area. Captain there is an opaque dome covering whatever is there."

"Use the tractor beam and lift the dome," Vax said.

The computer said, "Initiating tractor beam."

"We are being pulled out of orbit sir and the dome is rupturing," said the science officer.

"Halt tractor beam immediately," said Vax. "Prepare for our transport into the dome."

"That may be unwise Captain Vax, we don't know what is in the dome," said Amar. "Transport me first to know if it is safe."

"I am the man, the person responsible for all life, transport me instead," said the Man.

"I think we all four should go," said Shanta. "If we die we die together. We can't afford to lose one of us, with one of us lost it's like everything lost."

"I've decided, since the four of you cannot lose one of you because of grief, I will send all four of you together," said Vax.

"Man, Shanta, Amar, Prem, follow this unit to the transport room," said Vax.

The unit was suspended in the air and had the form of a cube. There was blinking lights around the side and the bottom indicating that it was operational. It must have been linked to the ship's computer since a screen on the communication console was plotting its movement.

The unit guided the four of them to the rear of the ship. They were fitted with atmospheric protection suits and communication equipment and were given some energy bars if they got hungry. After that they stepped to the left and entered the transport room.

The captain asked them if they were ready and they said yes over the intercom. "Since the four of you are ready, we are now going to transport you into the dome," said Vax, moving a lever.

"Clear area. Transport sequence initializing," said the computer. There was the sound of a noticeable hum. "Transport now complete, target has been reached, process has ended."

Captain Vax used the intercom to communicate with the bridge asking them if the landing party was okay.

"Captain we are receiving a beacon that indicates they are in a subterranean area inside the dome," said the communications officer. "Communication with them cannot be established."

"I am coming to the bridge," said captain Vax.

Captain Vax took the turbo lift and walked through several corridors to the bridge. "Is the beacon moving?" Said Captain Vax to the communications officer.

"It is moving fast at a linear rate captain. That would indicate that they are being transported buy a vehicle," said his communications officer. "If they were walking their rate would be irregular."

Vax said, "Why aren't we receiving communication from their radios?"

The communications officer said, "Captain Vax, their radios must have been taken away since I believe they must have been abducted."

A message came over the comm panel, "Captain Vax of the ship Criterion, we are the aliens from what should have been the Mars colony and have been monitoring your activities. We have a vessel in the dome and have located your search party. We want to know if we can have your permission to assist them?"

"Of course aliens, any help would be greatly appreciated," said Captain Vax. "What is their status aliens?"

Anticipating a yes answer, "We have beamed them from our primary detention holding vessels to the secondary vessel and is now in search of the cross," said one of the Mars aliens. "They are not considered a threat."

The Man, Shanta, Prem and Amar were very happy to be rescued. The Mars aliens were very understanding and could relate to their concerns. The aliens were scanning the area and identified a location where there were opposing forces that created a short of forward and reverse time. They could not penetrate that area with the ship's sensors.

The man said, "I believe there is something volatile that is biological at that area aliens. I'm going to instruct the heart computer to scan that area."

"Data H0," (The heart computer) said the man, "Scan the area in question at the year zero and report what you have discovered."

"Man, there is a body next to the cross that is alive and the cross is still erected," said Data H0. "After executing a count of beta radiation of carbon-14 I have determined that that identity is the Christ and also that cross was which he was crucified on. It is my recommendation that you separate the beams of the Cross to stop the anomaly of time at the vortex. This would also stop the expansion of the universe due to the love by God."

"Mars aliens," said Captain Vax, "We are sending a robot into the vortex to separate the cross and to recover the body of Jesus."

"You will need guidance," said the Mars aliens. "We will track your robot into the area."

"Mars aliens, the robot will be ready for deployment in 5 minutes," sad Captain Vax.

After six minutes, the cargo bay opened and the robot was deployed. Telemetry to the Mars alien ship was established and the commencement of tracking began.

"Logic control of the robot has been established Captain Vax," said a transmission from the Mars alien vessel. "The Robot is entering the atmosphere of Jupiter captain Vax, structural integrity has been maintained."

"The robot is approaching the dome captain Vax. We are now firing weapons to breach the dome... The dome has been breached and the robot has entered. The Robot has been programmed to disassemble the cross and to retrieve the Christ." Said the Mars aliens to captain Vax.

"Very well," said Captain Vax.

"The target has been reached Captain Vax and disassembly of the Cross has occurred," Said the Mars aliens.

Ronald A Arjune

134

Chapter 17

Meanwhile at Canis Majoris, the star stabilized and the universe stopped expanding. Captain Vorlon asked communications officer Valerie to prepare a message to Captain Vax, saying what has occurred. God was no longer experiencing love but a lot of anxiety and fear. This is due to a continuous decision for control.

"Please stop this Captain Vorlon, I need love," said God.

"Love is your sin God. It has to stop and stopped now," said Captain Vorlon.

God began to dematerialize and disintegrate into nothingness. "Help me please. I have to survive, don't let me die," said God.

Sensing an opportunity, Mother Lakshmi entered God and stopped the physical constants and was released a second time from God as the holy spirit and homed in on Anthony once again. Anthony was not experiencing anxiety.

"My creator it's been so long, God held me a prisoner for so long-over 2000 years." Said mother Lakshmi to Anthony. " A lot of destruction must have occurred in the universe. There is so much distress on your face creator."

"The main thing is that you're okay now my consort, and you're with me." said Anthony. "Soon that distress on my face will vanish."

Soon enough God died and Valerie sent the message to Captain Vax.

I have received your message Commander Vorlon," said Captain Vax. We have disassembled the cross and has retrieved Christ to the Criterion. He is now recovering. Love has been permanently stopped and the universe is well again.

Since God was dead and darkness was no longer restricting light, the man's heart computer data-H0 instructed the brain computer mc10-2b on the moon to perform the difference of light levels subtraction on the moon and that enabled the goddess of sexuality Kali to see and in the process the daughter of Anthony was detected by Kali interfaced as moon matter. The cancellation of light levels destroyed the power of lucifer, who made light impure, and Kali was able to rescue her. "Please come back to earth soon father, I will be waiting to see you." Said Anthony's daughter through KALI's voice.

The Man, Shanta, Prem and Amar were very happy now and everybody aboard captain Vorlon's ship were rejoicing. The search party of four returned to the Criterion. It was an awesome sight to them seeing the robot disassemble the cross.

Meanwhile in the infirmary of the Criterion the Christ was receiving saline solution from the ship's doctor for dehydration. They tried to communicate with him but he was unresponsive. After about 15 minutes he opened his eyes and in a sense of wonder asked where he was: "Where am I-who are you all?"

The ship's doctor said to him, "You are safe my Lord. You are aboard the ship Criterion, you have been rescued from Jupiter. Everything will be okay."

The Lord said, "What is Jupiter?"

A ship's doctor said, "Jupiter is a planet of the solar system of Earth where you have been crucified on by God."

"Where is the holy ghost, I gave up the holy ghost?" Said Christ.

"The holy ghost was used for love by God, he has been terminated and the holy ghost is free again in the universe along with the 5th Vedas." Said the Doctor.

Irony of God

END

137